JENNA & JONAH'S
FAUXMANCE

JENNA & JONAH'S FAUXMANCE

Emily Franklin & **Brendan Halpin**

BLOOMSBURY

LONDON BERLIN NEW YORK SYDNEY

Bloomsbury Publishing, London, Berlin, New York and Sydney

First published in Great Britain in March 2011 by Bloomsbury Publishing Plc
36 Soho Square, London, W1D 3QY

First published in the USA in 2011 by Walker Publishing Company
a division of Bloomsbury Publishing Inc
175 Fifth Avenue, New York, NY 10010

A CIP catalogue record of this book is available from the British Library

ISBN 978 1 4088 1630 1

Printed in Great Britain by Clays Ltd, St Ives plc, Bungay, Suffolk

1 3 5 7 9 10 8 6 4 2

www.bloomsbury.com

For Adam, costar of my favorite romance
—E. F.

To my parents, who gave me the gift of theater
—B. H.

1

NOT THAT YOU CARE

CHARLIE

I will never like a boy like Fielding Withers (and, yes, I know I used the word "like" twice in one sentence, but meaning different things). If there's anything I'm aware of, it's the words that come out of my mouth, since half the time I don't choose what they are.

Fielding Withers, known to the better part of the world as Jonah Jacobs, sits to my right in a chair with both names on it. One could make the argument (and I have) that he needs JONAH and FIELDING written in block letters because reading isn't his strong suit, but he probably needs both because he's not smart enough to know who he is at any given time.

"So are we gonna make out or what?" Fielding asks like he's trying to get me to pass the ketchup.

I shrug. "Depends. You think Bret Huckley'll be there?" We are forever being chased by legions of paparazzi—on the way to the set, at the Grind (our coffeehouse of choice),

1

shopping on Melrose, getting pedicures (me), biking to the Santa Monica Pier (Fielding), or running (both of us, side by side, agent's orders). But Bret Huckley is the worst. He's known for snagging shots when you're down and really out— like if your mom's having surgery, he's there in the waiting room, or if the spray tan goes horribly wrong, he's the first to sell the snaps to tabloids. And he's been on our case ever since rumors started about this being the last season of *Jenna & Jonah*.

And the thing is, the rumors might be true.

Cut to three years ago: I was fourteen. Fielding was fourteen and a half. The Family Network was going under—no one wanted their weird pet shows anymore (I mean, honestly, are *you* interested in watching tiny Maltese dogs learning to do ballet? No. It's beyond creepy)—so they tried one last thing. We were the last thing. *Jenna & Jonah's How to Be a Rock Star* premiered to, like, three people. But word got out and pretty soon more people—like, maybe twelve—were watching. By day, Jenna and Jonah, next-door neighbors who are perpetually on the verge of falling in love, were your average straight-A, car-wash-for-charity-organizing teens. But come night, they (and by "they" I mean we) rock. So we had mild success. Not bad for a former child star (me) and a total hick (Fielding).

"I think we should go for the arm around the waist. You carry this," Fielding says and thrusts a thick block of paper at me.

"What's this? The Great American Novel?" I sneer, because the last thing in the world this boy could do is write, even though he swears one day he will. He can't even leave a note that says more than three words, and those are limited to "Coffee," "Meet me," or his signature "Outta here."

Fielding pushes his hair—really a cocoa brown but now carefully streaked with very real-looking blond since we're shooting summer scenes—out of his eyes. He puts his hand on my arm and I fight the urge to flinch. "I *will* write that book someday," he says in his best believable voice. Sometimes he's so convincing it's hard to believe he's full of shit. "But this is a prop."

I check it out. It's the weight and size of a script, complete with *Jenna & Jonah's How to Be a Rock Star: Season 5* written perfectly. I check the time. We're due for our next scene in a few minutes—one where we sing a duet, a love song called "Not That You Care" that's already been leaked online and is rising in download popularity. The lyrics are pure mush—"You're so sweet," "How come you can't be mine," "I'll find you wherever you are," and so on—which, if you ask me, is totally creepy, because it makes love sound like stalking. Plus, we're just fake neighbors—how far apart could we be? But people have a hard time remembering that.

Cut to two and a half years ago. I'm fourteen and a half, and Fielding is fifteen and taller now, his shoulders a bit more broad, his face decidedly appealing. And the show's fine. It's okay. Then—I swear it might have been overnight (that's what

3

the tabloids claimed, anyway)—it happened. I got boobs. One headline read, "C Track Run," in honor of my name, Charlie Tracker, and my unfortunate jogging-bra issues. Before there could be more doubt about the realness of said breastage, my mom (then my manager, as well as a B-movie actress herself), went on E! saying it's genetic, look at her, showed her old school photos, and, sure enough, everyone's convinced. And they *are* real. But what isn't real is this: everything else.

"So we'll do the song, I'll grab my stuff, and let's just do the walk 'n' snug." Fielding and I lock eyes—his are green; mine are normally blue but I have brown contacts in. I'm probably the only actress around here with naturally blond hair. Another real thing, I guess. But producers felt that the blond/blue-eyed thing was too beachy, too cliché (but somehow next-door neighbors who fall in love aren't?), and that I was perceived as "warmer" with brown eyes. So my fake brown eyes look back at Fielding's green ones and we agree. The walk 'n' snug it is.

Cut to the end of Season 1. *Jenna & Jonah's How to Be a Rock Star* has picked up viewers after the boob buzz, so when our agents wake up Fielding and me in the middle of the night and tell us to meet them at four a.m. at the Twilight Diner in West Hollywood, we figure it's about a salary increase. Or a summer special—*Jenna & Jonah's Summer Splash* or something. What we got instead was a cheap cup of watery coffee with no soy milk anywhere in sight and an ultimatum: fall in love or fall apart.

So we chose love.

Or it chose us.

And we've been faking it ever since. Because even if the ratings were climbing courtesy of my breasts, they would fade like overwashed denim if we didn't give the audiences something more to cling to than cotton candy songs and stilted dialogue. Fake romance wins a lot of followers.

"You hear we're number two in Japan?" Fielding swigs water from a plastic bottle that he will later throw out before leaving the set with his camera-ready refillable eco-friendly metal bottle.

I nod. "Martinka told me," I say. Martinka's my agent and texts me every three to six seconds about any and all news. My thigh buzzes and I check the text. "Correction. Number one." Fielding reacts as though I've told him I like his socks (which I don't, because they're Jonah's socks, and therefore polka-dotted to accent Jonah's quirky style that is now showcased in every mall around the country).

"Yeah. Number one." He swigs the water again and then hands it to me. "You want this?" I'm about to be just the slightest bit touched—he remembers I get parched in the midafternoon. "It tastes like crap."

I nudge him and then water spills on his shirt. He jumps up, flailing like he's on fire, and assistants rush to his aid. "Don't even think of the walk 'n' snug now," he threatens, his green eyes glaring, his wet shirt clinging to his sculpted chest.

"Oh, like you have a choice," I say and then am quickly aware of the crew paying too much attention to our spat. I raise my eyebrows and Fielding Withers does his best Jonah smile—plump lips with just a little bit of teeth—and opens his arms wide. I know the drill. I know this choreography of love. So I step forward, letting him embrace me, while the crew breathes a collective sigh.

Aren't they sweet?

Cut to headlines: "Track and Field! Jenna and Jonah's Real-Life Love"; "Getting on Track—Charlie Leaves Her Wild Past Behind"; "Fielding Withers and Charlie Tracker—So in Love!!"

It's not difficult, really. I mean, they hold hands, the guy touches the girl's hair, the girl whispers something in his ear at the awards show, he fixes her dress strap on the red carpet, and you throw in some "candid" shots of them at the beach, go-carting, and, most recently, on vacation in Tahiti. Now that was fun: Fielding Withers—the boy of few words—a supposedly deserted island, and fish. Not exactly my version of a good time. I spent most of my days reciting Shakespeare to the marine life. I'd snorkel and rehearse lines for the ultimate play—*Much Ado About Nothing*. Everyone always obsesses about *Romeo and Juliet*: the words, the poetry of forbidden love, real love, love so deep it destroys you, and so on. But to me, *Much Ado* has it all: the banter, the hidden emotions, love tucked away like the secret you can't tell for fear it will ruin you. That's what I recited on Tahiti and all of

6

it would wash away in the water, where no one could hear it. I know every line of that play. Memorizing comes easy for me. The part about getting in touch with your true feelings, not so much. That's the price of Jenna and Jonah. No one can see us as anyone else.

We keep hugging. We're known for our long hugs. And I'm used to Fielding's smell—one part sweat, one part Sweet Teen cologne, which he has to wear since he's the face of their campaign. Three years and I still loathe the scent of it.

"It's time to sing," Fielding says into the top of my hair.

The stage is set. Makeup comes in and pats my chin and forehead with powder, touches up Field's hair.

I drop the fake script for Season 5 in my chair and can already imagine the walk 'n' snug. We perfected the move and coined the phrase way back in Season 1: arms around each other's lower back, Field moves his right hand just to my rib cage—all innocent, no feeling-up allowed—I laugh, snuggling into his shoulder, and he whispers something into my ear. Cheese. Smile. Snap. Photographers love it. Only this time I'll be holding the script for everyone to see, so everyone knows that yes, there's another season; no, we haven't been canceled; no, no problems on set with a director who is checking into rehab; no parent managers who take all the money and spend it; and, no, for the last time, we are not breaking up. We will walk 'n' snug and convince everyone that everything's fine. And for that moment, caught on film, it will be easy to believe.

2

ASK ME MY NAME

FIELDING

My mom picked Fielding because of *Tom Jones*. The book, not the singer. And Withers because of Bill Withers. The singer. Her favorite.

Aaron Littleton just doesn't sound like a leading-man name. It sounds like the name of the guy who plays the wise-cracking sidekick. Which is funny, because Nebs, my wisecracking sidekick on the show, is actually played by a guy named Hunter Davenport.

Hunter parties way too hard. I think he'll be dead by the age of twenty-five. I could be wrong.

I don't mean to sound cold. It's just the way stuff happens. You do too many drugs, you wind up dead one way or the other. Even in my hometown, Cincinnati. Which is most certainly not where we are now.

Now we're on our way to sip lattes photogenically, then a

little hand-in-hand walk on the beach—just about every third ocean-view house between the pier and Venice Beach has a webcam streaming live pictures. So we'll be downloaded a lot—we'll probably see some packs of tweens who will take cell phone pictures with us and put them on their Facebook pages. Free publicity. Keep the ratings up. All part of the job.

I have to say the job is starting to wear on me. I'm starting to wonder how much money is enough. I'm not quite set for life, but I figure by the time the DVD money stops flowing, our fans will have kids of their own and will shell out enough for reunion tour tickets and merch that we can slink back into obscurity and then retire comfortably.

And I'll never have to see her again.

Not that I hate Charlie. In another lifetime, I probably would have been one of those guys who secretly watches our very tween-centric show just to ogle Charlie. She's not only pretty, she's also funny as hell—or, anyway, she makes our lame scripts seem funnier than they actually are. She carries the comedy aspect of the show on her back. I carry the shaggy-haired-and-nonthreatening-eye-candy-for-the-tween-girls aspect. And it's pretty easy work. The scripts aren't very demanding, mostly just reshuffling our catchphrases week to week, and the songs are made so that any eleven-year-old can sing along.

But the fake romance—my second job, really—gets harder

every day. Sometimes I'll do stuff like whisper, "You've got spinach between your teeth," when we're posing for a "candid" picture.

Probably that stuff's mean.

No. I *know* it's mean. And I should feel bad. But, you know, as Sartre said, "Hell is other people." I can't actually use that quote in public because it would give the impression that I read books. I can't appear to be too brainy. Though, if I'm honest, I only read that one because my studio tutor made me.

But Charlie does put me through hell. And not just me. I guess the nice thing to call her is a perfectionist. Whenever the director sets up anything she doesn't like or the poor writers write something she doesn't like, she gets them to change it. She's really quite persuasive. They tried standing up to her at first, but she can throw a diva fit like you wouldn't believe. "I *respect* the audience, Jay! They *identify* with my character, and they're going to be *heartbroken* if she says this! I read the chat boards to find out what the fans want!" And she really does. Every day she's on her laptop checking out what everyone in the world is saying about us. When I'm feeling charitable, I think it must be exhausting to care that much.

The crew looks at me, pleading, whenever shooting is delayed because Charlie feels like some part of the show doesn't fit her personal vision. "You're her boyfriend," they seem to say. "Can't you do something?"

But I'm not her boyfriend. I just play her boyfriend in the

reality show we call real life. Not that I have a real life. But it's okay. I mean, my dad worked forty hours a week at the GE plant for twenty-five years before getting laid off, and now he fixes cars under the table. I paid off the house and I could easily support them, but being supported by his teenage son is not something my dad figures a man should do. So I devote 168 hours a week to this—well, minus the fifty-six hours, more or less, I spend sleeping—for five years, and then I'm set for life. I'll attend a small liberal arts college and maybe become a science-fiction writer. Or, you know, just get a little house on the beach (yeah, my dreams of a simple life don't really include going back to Cincinnati) and read, maybe learn to surf, and just not have anyone telling me where I have to go or what I have to do anymore.

Like right now. I attempt to order a medium iced latte, but Charlie interrupts, whispering through clenched teeth. Most people would think this is a smile, but I know it's a threat display. "Field. Did you hear me order a large? You can't be consuming fewer calories than me. Think for a minute, will you? They'll start taking telephoto shots of my thighs and making me into some horrible 'before' picture. We've talked about this."

Actually, she's talked. I've only listened. And usually not even that. "He'll have a large with *extra* whipped cream," she says to the leering barista. He catches me looking at him checking out her chest and looks guiltily at the floor. Dude, I want to say, you can have her. Take my girlfriend, please.

And then I could get a real girlfriend. We've now got fans who went through high school with us, attractive female fans of legal age. And I can't get near them. Because—George Orwell was wrong, you know (*1984* was another studio tutor–required classic)—it's *little* brother who's always watching you, and you never know who's got a cell phone camera aimed at you or who's going straight to the tabloids with the "My Wild Night with Cheating Fielding" story. My mom warns me about this particular danger pretty often. Usually right after Dad asks me which hot female celebrities I've met.

If I ever did become a front-page tabloid story like that, I'd be the one who derailed the gravy train—and the one who broke the heart of America's sweetheart, killing my likability and, therefore, my career.

Don't think I haven't thought about it. But then I remember all the time my mom put into taking me to auditions and rehearsals, and I feel bad about how I would let her down. And once, when even that guilt wasn't working, I went over the financials with Marjorie, my accountant. She says that with the market in the toilet, I'm getting great value on my investments right now, it's a great time to buy, and I shouldn't worry about all the paper value my stocks have lost. And my real estate. She says I could retire today, but I saw what happened to my dad, and I want a little extra security. Still, I sometimes think about ending it all with one bold stroke.

I actually think about it all the time. Two girls from USC

just sent e-mail through the fan page with photos attached and thoughts on just exactly how they'd like to get to know me listed in excruciating detail.

I'm only human, after all.

And so is Charlie. I think. She hides her humanity under a robotic control-freak exterior. Walking with our iced lattes in hand toward Santa Monica, she snuggles into the crook of my arm and I pull her close—like I need to protect *her* from anything, but, whatever, it's camera friendly—as some guy with a camera lens as long as his arm takes our picture from a block away.

"I could be in a dorm room at USC right now doing unspeakable things to girls named Brandi and Brittani," I say, smiling with practiced affection. "Not with *y*'s. With *i*'s."

"You smell like a sixth-grader on his way to his first dance who couldn't cover up his stink even with too much of Daddy's cheap cologne," she retorts, smiling up at me like I'm the only man in the world.

It's all I can do not to laugh. It's the cologne I promote. "Hey," I joke, "I paid nearly five bucks for this at the Rite Aid down the street!"

"Filling out an application for a job you're actually qualified for?" Charlie retorts.

"No, checking out this week's *Celeb Weekly* for details from your plastic surgeon on your enhanced—"

"You'll never get any closer to them than a magazine article, loverboy." Charlie smiles.

"Well, I've got your mom's, so I'm all set. Where do you want to do the script-reading shot? The pier?" The pier is a great place for paparazzi shots because of the Ferris wheel and roller coaster in the background reminding people of fun and adolescence. Still selling the Family Network brand. Also, we're close to the pier, and once we get the shot I can go home and not be Fielding till we get up and do it all again tomorrow. I think we're scheduled for a pancake-house breakfast before shooting. I'll have to check my calendar.

"We've done too many shots on the pier. Let's go to the farmer's market. We'll get some organic strawberries and do the shot there."

"Okay." It's away from the beach, which is going to add to the time we have to spend together this afternoon, but I like fresh produce as much as the next guy. I'll "surprise" her with some fresh sunflowers while she's buying strawberries; then we'll sit there with "images of youth and fertility" (a direct quote from our Family Network publicity training) and look at the Season 5 script. Which is a mock-up created by my agent. But hopefully a "they're just like *us*!" photo with us eating strawberries and laughing over the hilarious script will force the network to renew us for another season. This is the theory, anyway.

I really don't know if I want it to work or not.

3

"OVER" IS A FOUR-LETTER WORD

CHARLIE

Dahlias bright as pinwheels, yellow marigolds, purple irises pointing to the afternoon sun, apricot roses bunched together with raffia ribbons, and the dreaded sunflowers.

"Don't get the same ones today," I whisper to Fielding as we pass the flower cart and smile for a couple of teens and their moms, who try to act nonchalant but are in fact swooning over catching us in person. He's not a bad person, not slimy like so many Hollywood boys, but he's full of himself. So full there's no room for anyone else in there.

Fielding leans in, his lips close to my ear as though he's discovered my lobes are made of chocolate and he needs a taste. "Despite your wishes, you can't control my every move. If they had a Venus flytrap, believe me, I'd snag that for you and present it on one knee for all the world to see." I pinch his side and he flinches, then catches himself and laughs as though it tickled. "You give new meaning to the words 'ball and chain.'"

I pull back and, because of the sun's glare, only he can see my eyes squinting angrily behind my Wayfarer sunglasses. "I wouldn't touch your ball or chain if you paid me."

This is normal stuff, our usual back-and-forth, but for some reason Fielding doesn't end it with a kiss on the cheek and send me on my way to buy strawberries. Instead, his voice is low, seething. "From what I hear, you've touched enough balls that two more wouldn't make a difference."

My pulse races. I sweep my hair back from my face and gather it in a messy ponytail, securing it with an elastic I keep around my wrist. A woman and her friend linger close to us, clearly wanting to hear what I say next. And what should I say? That all the tabloid rumors about hooking up with James Linden or Asher Piece were nothing but air? The sun warms my shoulders but my arms feel riddled with goose bumps.

Snap! A photographer steps out from behind the flower cart and gets a few shots before we have time to collect ourselves. I quickly smile, put my hand in my bag as though I'm searching for something, and come up with my phone. I put it to my ear even though no one's there. "Oh, sure! Great news," I say into the empty phone. I wave faux-excitedly to Fielding, who looks positively bored and begins plucking petals from a fuchsia-colored dahlia and flinging them to the ground, where they land like drops of blood. "We're number one in Sweden!" I hold up my finger in the one position and the photographer, satisfied with his shots, skulks away.

Under my breath I say, "You're a dick," to Fielding. He looks at the ground and, for a moment, looks truly sorry. I crumple like tinfoil when I see that look; it's endearing, loveable. Once, back in Season 1, we had to do this scene where I taught him to dance. We kept messing up and it was early enough on that we weren't a fake couple, and I might— might—have had the smallest of crushes on him. So we hung out by choice, trying to get the steps right. But the funny thing was that he can dance, really well, actually. And I'm as coordinated as a drunk flamingo in furry boots—which is to say not at all. So he taught me off camera but I taught him on. I almost bring this up, but before I can he waves to someone. I turn to see who it is. James Linden, fellow teen star and notorious scenester who lives to love them and leave them. Or not so much love as *lust*. Then again, he's an indie film favorite, so he's allowed to be unshowered and gritty, sleazy but sexy. *Jenna & Jonah* is a family show and we have to "uphold the values and lifestyle to which the Family Network is committed" (a quote from my contract).

"Hey, loser!" James shouts in our general direction.

"I'm taking off," Fielding says to me, pushing his hair back from his eyes. He's gorgeous in the sun and I swallow hard to avoid noticing the way sunlight glints off his hair, the easy way he moves his body, as though he's always just stepped away from a massage table. Which maybe he has.

"What about the shot with the script?" I ask, trying not to whine, but I don't want to deal with Martinka's wrath if more rumors circulate about problems on set or the show's future.

"You'll survive without me." Fielding grins. Who knows what he and James will go do. No doubt some secret boys' club meeting that I'm excluded from: girls, drinks, driving fast—all activities prohibited by our network.

I turn his ambivalence into a quoteworthy moment. "How can I survive without you?" I ask and stand on tiptoe to kiss him. It's a peck on the lips, nothing more, standard stuff, and I can feel Fielding try not to wince.

A few paparazzi take note of our cute farewell and then leave me alone. I wander around halfheartedly, picking up sprigs of lavender and smelling them. I consider buying a bunch of cheese but then remember I'm not allowed to have it by order of my dermatologist, so I create a fantasy meal instead. When I was growing up, my grandma cooked giant meals—huge spreads of sautéed onions and fresh pasta, crisp green beans with shallots and garlic, cheese tarts, and double-layer chocolate chip brownies for dessert. I haven't had anything like that in years. Not just because Martinka and everyone around me monitors my every mouthful, but because I have no time. And no place to cook. Sure, I own my house, but it's pretty much for show. There are no pots or pans in the state-of-the-art kitchen cabinets, because I never need them. Takeout, restaurants, on-set dining, awards shows, catering truck—that's how I eat. But I miss it. Sometimes I wonder if I could still do it, remember the recipes my grandma made me, or if those, like so much, are just distant memories of another life.

"Jenna, look over here!"

I automatically look up, even though I feel inclined to point out, "I'm not Jenna!" This is said with a cheery smile, of course, and I catch none other than Bret Huckley, infamous paparazzo complete with his multiple cameras, lenses capable of capturing the insides of your pores.

"Charlie Tracker, why on earth are you alone?" Bret asks while simultaneously snapping picture after picture of me in case I suddenly falter. He lives for catching stars at their weakest, getting paid six figures or more for proof of failure.

"A girl needs some private time," I say, hoping he quotes me on that and Fielding reads it and translates it to mean "away from my crappy fake boyfriend."

"So, you're not fighting with Fielding?"

I shake my head and choose the perfect pint of strawberries—deep red, small, local, and sweet-smelling. I hand the seller ten dollars even though they cost half that and walk away toward a grassy patch where I can sit and attempt to enjoy my limited free time.

Just doing simple things like sitting on the grass, feeling the breeze on my legs makes me feel so relaxed I could fall asleep if it weren't for fear of someone making fun of me for it. Nearby, a toddler tugs on her mother's hat and the mom slips it on her little head. Adorable. I was the same age when I made my first commercial: Li'l Huggeroos, the diapers that don't leak. Let me say for the record, they do leak. I know this because Lulu Lichtman, my first agent, kept a journal of everything that happened and let me read it the day my mother demanded I switch to Martinka, power agent to the A-list. You'd think my mother would have been the one keeping a journal, charting her only kid's path to fame, but my mother was too busy securing my next gig (Twinkle Toes, the shoes for every young princess) to bother. I became legally emancipated at fifteen after I discovered that my parents had drained my bank account to finance a chain of workout studios for pets, which went bankrupt, and then took up acting and sent me the bills for their lessons. I bought my own house right away, and even though I don't cook in it, it's mine. I never wanted to act—my parents were the ones who saw me as their gravy train and pushed me into auditioning before I could speak. And then, well, I just got enmeshed in the machine. It's difficult to step off the fame track, mainly because now I don't know what I would do or who I'd be without a script. The simple pleasures I always used to enjoy—cooking, singing without an electronic keyboard and background tracks—aren't a part of my schedule anymore. Even the farmer's market isn't mine to really enjoy.

"Oh, honey, don't take the nice girl's strawberries,"

the toddler's mother warns and follows her child as the girl grabs a whole handful of fruit and squishes it in her small palm.

"It's okay." I laugh and dig in my bag for a tissue. "Here." I give the mom the tissue and she thanks me.

"It's amazing the stuff she gets into. Thanks for not freaking out," the mom says.

"No problem," I tell her and pick one of the nonmushed berries up and hold it by the stem, eating with abandon as the toddler does the same. "I'd never finish the whole pint anyway, so have some."

The mom reaches in and sits down near me. It's so nice. A normal, peaceful interaction.

I give it four seconds before it implodes.

"Berries are always so good this time of year. I should really get some on the way out," the mom mutters as her child smears red juice all over her face.

"The best ones are Fleischer's, the last stall on the left," I tell her, wishing Fielding had stayed with me. Not just for the snapshots but for company. Three. Two.

"Oh, really? I'll have to—"

One.

She looks at me, seeing me for the first time instead of just being embarrassed about her toddler's sticky hands. "Oh. God. You're . . ."

I nod. "It's okay." Like somehow it's worse for me to

21

have a strawberry stolen than it is for a regular person? "Really."

The mom blushes, and starts stammering. "It's just . . . even though I'm not your demographic, really, I'm still—I'm a huge fan. I mean, *huge!* The duet—that one on the beach with the waves and the hula dancers doing backup . . . ?"

" 'Say It Isn't a Summer Thing,' " I answer. In a moment of on-set camaraderie, Fielding and I made up an inappropriate song entitled " 'Over' Is a Four-Letter Word," which had us doubled over with laughter, using every word forbidden to Jenna and Jonah while we pushed each other off a cliff as we simultaneously gave the finger to each and every paparazzi onlooker. But "Say It Isn't a Summer Thing" was *the* anthem two springs back, the song you hear so much you can't help but know every word. I wore an uncomfortable sarong during the shoot. It left a welt on my lower back that hurt more than Fielding saying I'd be lucky to be anyone's summer anything. The truth is, he's exactly the kind of guy I would want to date if I lived in the real world, which to me seems as far away and made up as our own *Jenna & Jonah* set. They screen-tested loads of boys, and I hardly noticed, but when they played Fielding's tape—he juggles in it, which wasn't scripted—I couldn't stop grinning. I didn't know the producers were watching my reactions to the screen tests, and it was more than a little embarrassing when they offered Fielding the part and showed him a tape of me watching his audition.

The mom claps. "Exactly!" Her phone is in her hand before I can say anything else. "Could you just . . . one chorus? Anything?" She starts to hum and mumble-sing. "You! You flip-flopped my heart this summer . . . You're something something I can't remember the words . . . the one for me but . . . dadaaaa."

Such memorable lyrics. I politely decline and begin to gather my things. She'd film me and it would be on YouTube before I even got home to my empty kitchen. "Sorry. Nice meeting you, though," I say and pat the toddler on her head for good measure. In a normal life, I'd be the kid's baby-sitter.

The mom, once kind and chill, can't let me go. She tugs on my bag from her spot on the grass. "Oh, you're leaving?"

I pull on my bag, just enough to get her off and try to walk away. From normal to freako fan in the course of four seconds. Sometimes it's even shorter.

My bag, itself a product placement to try and land a spokesperson deal for Le Bon Sac, the French purse maker, clearly isn't worth the thousand dollars it costs retail, because the shoulder strap snaps, splattering everything in it onto the ground. Quickly, I grab as much as I can and shove it in: eyeliner, UltraGloss lip gloss (contractually obligated to carry on me at all times), phone, pager, other cell phone, directions to the random pancake house where I have to meet Fielding tomorrow at some ungodly hour for breakfast, a spare pair of flats, car keys, house keys, SuperFit! sports energy bar (my supposed "snack of choice" even though it tastes like sand)—all of this tossed in a jumble back into the bag.

"Forget something?" It's the voice of evil in the form of Bret Huckley.

I'm about to deny it when I see what he has in his hands. He dangles something between two fingers, stretching it out in front of him as though it's lingerie. *Jenna & Jonah's How to Be a Rock Star: Season 5*.

"That's mine," I say and snatch it back. But the damage is already done. He's snapped a picture of it with his micro-cam, the one permanently attached to his wrist.

"Of course," Bret says. "I wouldn't want you to be without your script."

I sigh. Maybe there's nothing juicy here. He got the shot we were hoping for, right? Season 5, everything's cool. At the bottom of each script it always says the same thing—"PROPERTY OF CHARLIE TRACKER/FIELDING WITHERS" (alphabetical)—and then the number of scripts that have been distributed, which is always only two—one for each—to prevent plot leaks to the press or online. Even camera and on-set crew have scripts only on the closed set. I swing my bag on my shoulder and start toward my car.

"Say, Jenna," Bret says a bit too loud. "I shouldn't over-interpret the fact that you're reading Season Five without Fielding, should I?"

Shit. Here's the juice.

I pivot and smile my widest. "Of course not! He's got a copy, I've got a copy, we're all set!"

Bret raises his bushy eyebrows and smirks.

I walk away. It's only when I look at the script in my hand that I notice the fine print at the bottom of the script: "PROPERTY OF CHARLIE TRACKER—Copies Distributed: 1." Fielding's name is nowhere to be seen.

★4★

IT'S OVER

FIELDING

Just driving down the boulevard in James's convertible is awesome. Wind's in my hair, and every time we stop the car, bikini-clad hotties literally squeal. We've been in God knows how many cell phone photos in the last ten minutes, and we've had six phone numbers chucked into our car. The crumpled pieces of paper sit in my lap. I suppose this is how Tantalus felt. Tormented forever in the Greek and/or Roman afterlife by being ankle deep in water that would drain away whenever he bent over to drink, and by tree limbs groaning with succulent fruit right in front of his face that would shoot out of reach whenever he tried to pick something. My studio tutor taught me that story right before I took the SAT.

It's where we get the word "tantalize"—to put something succulent (number 28 in *50 Power Words for the SAT!*), like that girl in the green bathing suit three traffic lights back, just out of reach. I can't call her—apparently her name is Holly—because I'm locked in fake love. And James won't call her because he's not interested.

"Thanks for rescuing me. I think I was about to strangle Charlie and thereby ruin my career."

"Thereby? Who says that?"

"Um. Me?"

"Bookworm."

"You know, it wouldn't kill you to read something once in a while."

"Yeah, well . . ." James smirks.

"In fact, you know what? Friends of the Library is having a book sale—let's stop by. We can get armloads of books. Last year I got twenty books for forty bucks."

"Sounds awesome, but I've got other plans."

"Ah, no. Come on, James. Let me out of the car. I'm not— I suffered through fake romance all morning; don't make me do fake friendship all afternoon."

James stops the car and looks at me. "Please, man. I need your help."

The car is still. I could hop out. I mean, I'm being used again. Still a pawn, but now I'm in a different game. I should have stayed with Charlie for another ten minutes. Then I could have gotten the shot and been done with it. Instead I'm sucked into more deception.

We've done this before. We'll pick up another young Hollywood B-lister, and a C-lister that James is inexplicably fond of. We'll make a big show of going into GameStop and buying the latest Xbox 360 releases. And then we'll be seen buying lots of chips and energy drinks.

The way this was pitched to me the first time—by my agent, Jo, after she took a lunch with James's publicist—was as a win-win. I get to be seen as a good influence on young Hollywood's bad boy—look! When he hangs out with Fielding, he plays video games and drinks energy drinks instead of clubbing till the wee hours! And James gets some alone time with Casper Harvey, the aforementioned other closeted B-lister. What really sold me on it, though, was this: it's the kind of thing that college students do on TV. I don't know if it's what they do in real life, but it makes me feel kind of collegiate, which keeps the full-time-student dream closer.

Yeah, so this is the big thing James and I have in common: we both have secret lives. Which is probably why we've come to be friends even though our friendship began as a publicity stunt. People think I'm secretly gay because I can sing and dance. Also, I do think some people might somehow get that my public canoodling with Charlie isn't completely on the level, and they assume this means it's a cover for *my* homosexuality.

James, on the other hand, is thought to be an insatiable womanizer and nightclubbing party machine. Despite the fact that, at nineteen, he's technically too young to get into clubs, he likes to get photographed leaving them with two girls at three in the morning; he's got permanent stubble and tousled hair; he couldn't sing if his life depended on it (as we discovered when we all played Rock Band for a couple hours before James and Casper's alone time a few months ago); and he and Casper are completely, cutely, disgustingly in love.

I don't mean disgusting like, "Ew, gross, they're guys"—I do work in Hollywood after all—I just mean disgusting like as soon as we get back to James's place, they get goofy and hand-holdy and start calling each other Snuggles. Yes. Now it can be told. James Linden, indie film stud and sex symbol to bespectacled college girls everywhere, calls Casper Harvey Snuggles.

I don't know why they don't just live together and pretend they're bad-boy roommates. And I don't know why the Xbox tournament is strictly necessary, but James's agent says having a boys' club that he hangs out with helps James sell the public on the idea that he's heterosexual. In any case, it beats the hell out of playing Xbox by myself, and it is nice to hang out with people besides Charlie. It probably gives me enough of a break to keep playing the role of her boyfriend.

Whatever the case, now we're outside the apartment occupied by Devin, who plays the oldest son on a sitcom on the CW that even his mom doesn't watch. James is honking the horn and my phone buzzes. *Jo*, my phone reads. Less than a year ago, before she went back to Cincinnati to devote her time to my little sister's gymnastics career, Mom put me in the care of an agent who appeared warm and folksy. Jo is about as warm and folksy as a cobra, but she did put on a good show during the time when Mom was here. Now that Mom's gone, the show is over.

"Yeah, Jo?"

"Fielding. Can you explain this Twitter stream I'm following? I saw a picture of you with a bosomy blonde leaning into your side of a convertible." *Bosomy*, she says. Like she's my grandma, though she's only forty.

"Fans, Jo. You know, they want—"

"I guess I'm just wondering why you're not at the farmer's market with Charlie getting the script shot."

"Well, I ran into James, and he invited me over to play Xbox."

"What about the shot?"

"Well, I figured—"

She gives a deep, heavy sigh. "Fielding. I had assistants making that fake script all day yesterday. I've got a call with the network first thing in the morning, which is why we needed to get those pictures out today. The negotiations are at a critical period, and I need you on board with our strategy. We talked about this, Field. I can't understand why you would sabotage yourself like this."

"Charlie's there with the script, I gave her sunflowers—"

"But you didn't get the shot."

"No. I guess not."

There's a long silence. Devin climbs into the backseat and fist-bumps both of us, and the car is moving again. Off to pick up Snuggles.

"Fielding. This is a very, very delicate time in the negotiations. I am going to need you to cooperate. You have to help me help you."

"Okay."

"Call Charlie. You guys need a romantic dinner out."

"Oh, for Christ's sake, Jo!"

"Field. Do you want my help here? I know you've been very good about saving your money, but I also know everybody's investments are in the toilet right now. My 401(k) isn't even worth 200K anymore." She waits for a laugh, and I give a little chuckle, though daily repetition hasn't improved this joke. "You need to work, I need you to work, and I think we've got at least one more season on the gravy train. Then I promise I will get you that indie comedy you want right after Season Five wraps. Okay?"

"Okay." Just one more season. Twenty episodes. Less than a year of my life until my life becomes mine. It doesn't seem too much to ask for—after all, I'll still be eighteen. The age when normal people graduate high school. I can go to college and be one of them. Except I'll never have to go work for people I hate doing stuff I hate like Dad did. If I can just pull off one more season of this.

"So call Charlie, will you?"

"Yes, ma'am." I've got stuff to say—the hell with you, the hell with Charlie, the hell with *Teen Scene* magazine, the hell with all of it. I don't say this, though. I may be an animal in a cage, but Dad was a cog in a machine for twenty-five years and he's got exactly nothing to show for it. I can be a caged animal for one more season.

"Good boy." I feel like she has just patted me on my head and given me a liver treat.

And the phone goes dead. I call Charlie, who informs me that Martinka tore her a new one and tells me when and where we're having dinner. Just as a gag, I ask, "What am I having?"

Charlie doesn't seem to get that I'm busting her chops. "You'll get the lemon chicken with couscous and seltzer from the bar, not mineral water in the bottle on the table."

I snort. "See you there."

She hangs up without saying good-bye.

"Sorry, everybody," I say to the car.

We pick up Snuggles, go buy *Extreme Robo-Football 3*, enough energy drinks and salty snacks to keep us wide awake and chap-lipped for a week, and head back to James's house.

The Xbox 360 tournament is unremarkable except that I actually win a game of *Extreme Robo-Football 3* against Casper, the Xbox king of young Hollywood. That and Devin is texting constantly, saying he's up for a part in the new Tarantino movie. Right before James and Casper retreat to the second floor, Devin says, "Yo, J"—Devin, a white kid, affects hip-hop slang in his personal life—"my sidekick is dying, yo. C'I check my e-mail on your computer, yo? I'ma hit up that casting director on AIM."

"Go nuts," James says and disappears up the stairs.

Devin installs himself in front of the computer, leaving me holding my controller and looking at the pause screen of *Extreme Robo-Football 3*. It's not much of a one-player game. I'd grab a book off the shelf to read but, of course, this being James's place, there are no bookshelves and no books. Just "media."

But, this being James's place, there is a deck with a chair that looks out at the ocean. I ease into the chair, close my eyes, and listen as the white noise of the traffic easing by blends with the white noise of the surf, and before I know it I fall into a dreamless sleep.

I wake up a while later feeling happy, hopeful, and refreshed. Maybe I just haven't been sleeping enough. Late at night is the only time that feels like mine, so I guess maybe I stretch it out too much.

"Hey!" I say as I open the glass sliders and enter the living room. The TV is off and Devin is not here. "Hello?" I look at the clock on the microwave: it's apparently six fifteen, and I'm supposed to meet Charlie at seven. I'm in someone else's house, unshowered and not dressed for having romantic dinner shots taken. And I don't have a car.

I call up the stairs, but there's no answer from either of the Snuggleses. And the Porsche is not in the driveway. Great.

I borrow a bike, ride the two miles to my place, throw on some free clothes that one of the lines I do ads for sent over, and go meet Charlie at À la Maison, the new French-Moroccan place with the maître d' in the red fez. Sadly, there are no belly dancers. A photo of me showing any interest at all in a belly dancer would be bad for the image. It's seven ten when I arrive, and Charlie's wearing a smile that looks like she wants to spit nails at me.

"Ten minutes late, snookums," she says. "People saw me standing there all alone and think there's a problem. That's how rumors start." Instead of sitting across from me, she sidles up next to me.

"Then gimme some tongue, baby," I say, pulling her in close for a deep kiss that has all the passion of a trip to the dental hygienist. My particular dental hygienist is a very attractive young woman, so the analogy holds: I know this is just professional, not personal, but it's kind of arousing anyway.

She does a great "almost overwhelmed by passion" face when she pulls away. I know it's disgust she's almost over-whelmed by, but I have to give her props. She is really good at acting like someone who's in love with me. So good that I almost fell for it once. Okay, twice. But those were embar-rassing incidents I'd rather not talk about.

I order what Charlie told me to, the preserved-lemon chicken with couscous. Charlie knows I'm a vegetarian but makes me order meat whenever she does. She has outlined five reasons for this, but I always stop listening at reason two. I just pick around whatever the dead beast is. Jo likes this, too—she's afraid that revealing what I really eat will make me seem "too crunchy" and make middle America distrust and hate me.

The waiter walks away, and I pretend not to notice as people pretend they're texting but actually hold the phones way too high and snap our pictures.

Confident that we've been photographed looking intimate, Charlie moves and sits across from me, and I hold her hand across the table while we wait for our food. My phone vibrates as a text from Jo comes through: *Dinner shots look great. Don't forget script.*

I gaze longingly into Charlie's eyes. "Got the script?"

"Of course, darling," she says. "Want to hold hands across the table and read it while we wait for our food? Won't that be adorable?"

"Certainly." I say, resisting the urge to check my phone to see what time it is, how much longer till I can get home.

We spend the next five minutes looking adorable, faces close together in the faux-Moroccan candlelight and reading the fake script, or rather pretending to read it, since it's mostly just stuff Jo's assistants cut and pasted from old scripts. It's not really that much worse than the usual scripts they give us.

Outside the window, a glint of reflected streetlight catches my eye. I see that the light's reflecting off a telephoto lens sticking out of Bret Huckley's car.

"Huckley in the house," I say, relieved that we'll be able to stop snuggling.

"Thank God," Charlie says. "I was about to pass out from sitting next to you. When's the last time you showered?"

She's probably got me there. I didn't have time to shower after biking home. I can't sniff my pits in public, but it wouldn't surprise me if I was a little ripe. "Yeah, your mom got me all sweaty. Sorry."

Charlie gives me a smile that appears genuine. "What's really funny about that is you think you're man enough to handle my mom."

"Ouch!" I say. The dead bird with preserved lemon and couscous arrives. Charlie has a roasted vegetable salad with a dainty portion of free-range organic chicken perched on top.

I take a bite of the stuff around the chicken. I guess it's good, but, you know, there's a dead bird in the middle of the plate. It kind of grosses me out. We did get some sweet mint tea, though, and I take a sip. It's delicious. I let it sit on my tongue, and then I'm glad I did. It's the last thing I'll ever taste as America's Top Teen Idol.

My phone rings at the same time as Charlie's, and we both pick up.

"What the hell do you mean, they know it's fake?" I hear Charlie saying in one ear, while in the other I hear Jo say this: "Great. We're into twenty-four-hour damage control. You've just been outed as part of James Linden's gay entourage."

"His what?" I ask. Jo tells me about pictures and e-mails that have just surfaced, obviously forwarded from James's computer by Devin, that out both James and Casper pretty convincingly. And since I was photographed with them all over town and I can sing and dance, well, as far as the gossip blogs are concerned, it's case closed.

I look at Charlie. She looks completely lost, and all I want to do is laugh. It's over. At last, it's finally over.

5

SNAPSHOT OF MY HEART

CHARLIE

"And this room here is the school set, which I'm sure you recognize," I say and motion toward the chairs-with-desks-attached all in neat rows in Mr. Spencer's global studies classroom. Global studies is the kind of class that only exists in television shows about high school, because it serves virtually no purpose except to give Jenna and Jonah a reason to tour the world and sing about it "for extra credit," which is kind of what I'm doing right now, with whatever her name is. "Sorry, what is your name again?"

"Nicki Kenny," she says and fixes her purple beret, the kind that Jenna wore this fall, making it an immediate hit at Target and all the chain stores. "It's easy to remember because it's two first names, really." She laughs and sits in one of the set desks as though she, too, is about to hear Mr. Spencer (played by Emmett Vestergaard in a somewhat humiliating return to the small screen after his previous award-winning turns on screen and stage) make some of his verbal quips about Scottish Highland plays and the "cool tunes" from Argentina.

"Nicki Kenny," I say and commit it to memory, if only for the next eight minutes, which is all I have until hell breaks loose. Or, correction, more hell breaks loose.

"Is this real?" Nicki asks and picks up a piece of chalk from the classroom set.

"Yes."

"And is this real?" She holds up a globe.

"Yup."

"And what about this? What is it?" She gushes about everything.

"That's an apple, and, no, it's not real. It's the one I bring to Mr. Spencer every day."

"So they just recycle the same apple?" She taps the side of it with her fingernails, amazed at the hollow sound. "I always thought it looked so good, like it made me want an apple to eat right then and there!"

I sigh and nod, wishing I could be elsewhere. Even pretending to care about this isn't challenging, just annoying. "Well, the prop department is excellent—they were up for an Emmy a while back."

"Oh my gosh—is this where Fielding Withers stood during that serenade?" Nicki clears her throat and starts singing like everyone always does. "No matter what map we're following, no matter which place we go, we're always together and forever, you know . . ."

"You have a nice voice," I say and I'm not lying for the first time in what feels like years. Probably *is* years. Nicki Kenny is the Family Network first-place award winner for some essay she wrote about how she's the biggest fan and her hometown of Nowheresville, USA, is the perfect place for Jenna and Jonah to visit because they're so something something—who knows. I didn't have to read the thing. I only have to give her a tour of the set.

"So when's Jonah coming?"

"Fielding," I automatically correct and start leading her toward the lockers. The hallway scenes are good for filler of crowds of students or for drama—if only I had a dollar for every time I slammed my locker in a fit of teen angst.

"Here's his room." I give up the pretense of not being exhausted and plop down on Jonah's bed. It was supposed to be me and Fielding giving this tour, but now that he's supposedly gay and agents and managers and the network are all freaking out, he somehow has the morning off and I'm left pointing out the details of our delusional days: This is where we pretended to go to junior prom! Here's my fake front stoop where my overprotective TV dad always interrupts us before I can actually kiss anyone and ruin the offscreen illusion of being pure enough to be sainted.

"So you guys share a bathroom?" Nicki asks.

"Well, I have my own—or Jenna has her own—but it's on the other soundstage. We just share this one and see—" I turn a fake wall around so now the bathroom is pink. "And they just take shots of whatever they need."

Nicki nods. "Me and my brothers do, too. Share a bathroom, I mean. I have three of 'em—they're all super sporty, so they smell, but, hey, it's kind of fun to go to their games."

"I imagine it would be," I say and lie back on Jonah's bed. It's actually comfortable, made up in neutral beiges that contrast with the navy blue rug and his teddy bear that he "just can't give up" so it travels on the road when Jenna and Jonah are supposedly playing to sold-out shows in Japan. When we actually played to sold-out shows in Japan, they had about forty of the same bears that they'd haul in and throw out to the crowd.

"Imagine?" Nicki sits down on the floor right next to me. I roll my head to the left so I can see her. "You mean, you've never been to a Mustangs game? Of course you haven't—what am I saying? The Mustangs are our local team and they've been league champs six seasons in a row and it would have been eight if Jake Dalton hadn't torn his ACL." She catches her breath and stands up. "What about your room?"

I sigh and feel sure that despite the quiet of the set, the closed lot, and the early hour, I can hear crowds swarming, photographers, newscasters, bloggers, everyone pooling because of him, because of me, because of us—or the lack of us. "Sure—it's through here."

"Not through the big hallway?" she asks and furrows her brow. Her bright red hair falls to her chin in an easy flip; her skin is lightly freckled.

"It's a set," I explain, deadpan and unable to hide my mood. "So, yeah, it's supposed to look like all the rooms are connected, but they're not. That hallway with the family portraits is way over there." I pull her along so she can see it, then my room, and then we'll be done. "A lot of the time they can't fit cameras into a tight space, like a real bathroom or a hallway that connects the rooms, so they just use whatever they want for establishing shots."

"Establishing shots," Nicki Kenny repeats.

"Yeah, it's a shot used at the beginning of a scene to establish where you are, or certain details—like, Jenna's in her room crying, and we see her through the bathroom and see her rock star wig on the counter in a heap."

"There are a lot of terms, huh?" Nicki Kenny picks up a bottle of shampoo from the bathroom. "Hey—it's empty." I raise my eyebrows. "Oh. A prop. I get it." She laughs and is so sweet and genuinely clueless I have to laugh, too. "You know, I'm not an idiot. I'm a total Jenonah fan, but I do, like, know other things . . ."

I wave her over to Jenna's dresser. On top are various school awards, a Grammy, and a heart-shaped picture of Jonah as a little kid. The set designers actually used a real photograph they got from Fielding. He's sitting on top of a beat-up faded blue pickup truck with an actual piece of hay sticking out of his mouth. If I didn't know better, I'd think he was cute.

"I'm captain of speech team, for one. And I'm the top seller three years running for school fund-raising tickets. And I work part-time at the local theater." She blushes. "It might seem small-time to you, but we put on some good productions—Ibsen's *Ghosts, Singin' in the Rain, Waiting for Godot*, which no one got and some people left partway through. We did *Guys and Dolls*, which was a huge hit even though Peter Frampton—who has the same name as some old rock star, but he isn't a rock star, he's a lame-ass sophomore— broke up with me the night before *Guys and Dolls* closed, so I was bummed."

My mouth hangs open. Not only because she talks more than I do, but because, even though she's here on the set of *Jenna & Jonah's How to Be a Rock Star*, she speaks normally. To *me* like I'm normal. As if I could be.

She stares at me through the mirror. Standing side by side, we're not that different. Not a different species. We even look little alike. My haircut probably cost more than her plane ticket here, and my clothing is cooler, and she should definitely lose the flared-sleeve cardigan and the beret, but otherwise . . .

"So what are you good at?" she asks me and bounces onto my twin bed. At home, I have a California king, which is pretty much like sleeping on a football field. Alone. I don't answer. "Jenna? I mean, sorry, Charlie?"

"Good at?" I lick my lips. I swear I hear crowds. Shouting. My heart pounds thinking about everything that waits outside this set. It was a haven, an escape. Come here, be Jenna, slide through with straight As, be popular, have a close relationship with parents who don't waste my hard-earned money on poker games or cosmetic surgery. It'd be an unrealistic family, maybe, these supportive parents, a brother who adores me, and the best boyfriend ever. So what if it's fake? I'd still be pulling in a hefty paycheck. Only now this set is a literal escape from the real life of news and what's going to happen to the show, to me and Fielding, to my future career. Beyond these walls is everything unscripted and I have no idea how to handle it.

"Come on, you must know something," Nicki Kenny encourages. She has her hands on her normal-sized hips and smiles. She comes from a place where parents go to football games and cheer their kids on, or buy tickets to their daughter's play even though she's not even in it and is just selling tickets. Where people have brothers they're truly proud of and normal things happen like getting dumped at a sucky time but without people recording your tears and broadcasting it on national TV that night.

"We should go," I say. "That's pretty much it. You didn't see the graduation set, but that's closed—they're doing bleacher work or something."

"You guys are graduating?" Nicki's voice is loud,

surprised, highlighting at once my mistake. You never tell what happens next. Confidential plot details.

"Nah, I was kidding," I say convincingly. I pull her away, distracting her from the season finale details. Jenna and Jonah *are* about to receive their diplomas, which means we'll lose the younger viewers unless we create a reason for keeping them around or we send everyone to the same made-up university that just happens to be down the street. It's all too complicated, so what'll happen is suddenly Mr. Spencer will announce to Jenna and Jonah that they never completed their final projects and missed too many classes, so they need to repeat senior year! What a surprise—one more season of big bucks and corporate sponsorship and kids falling in love with us.

We head to the back exit where I will hand Nicki Kenny from Nowheresville, USA, to my agent, Martinka, who will give her a signed poster and CD. She'll pass her off to Fielding's manager, who will get her a hat or something—maybe a T-shirt for each of her giant, sporty brothers to mop up their sweat or something.

"Here's the end of the tour," I say and give her a pat on the back.

Nicki Kenny does the unthinkable. She pulls me into a hug. She wraps her arms around me and says into my hair, "So what are *you* good at?"

I don't push away, because it's actually been a long time

since someone hugged me who wanted to. "Besides this?" I take a breath. "I know every line in Shakespeare's best play." I take another breath. "And I make amazing pasta sauces and brownies. Or I used to."

More noise from outside. Definitely not my imagination. I pull away and revert back to promotional mode. "Thanks for joining us on set!" Us? "I mean me."

"No, thank *you*! It was great." She grins and scribbles something down on a piece of paper. "Here's my contact info— just in case, you know, you're ever in the area and want to catch a show or a Mustangs game . . ."

I don't even know what area she means. It's just some- where in another universe without film festivals and there- fore not on my radar. The paper slides into my jeans, where it will live until I forget about it and it turns to shreds when my maid washes it. Then I hear more noise—this time, a clear shout.

"There is no access!"

There's a thud against the metal door where I'm stand- ing. Then the familiar buzz of Martinka bothering me with more bad news. She always writes in all caps, so her texts and notes read as though she's yelling at me. Which she probably is. *THE PUBLIC IS OUTRAGED. LE BON SAC HAS DROPPED NEGOTIATIONS FOR HAVING YOU AS THE FACE OF THEIR SUMMER CAMPAIGN. THE NETWORK IS CONSIDERING DROPPING JENNA & JONAH FROM THE FALL LINEUP.*

Before I even put the phone down, it buzzes again. "Oh, what now?" I ask aloud and click to find out. *MOB SCENE. WORSE THAN SYDNEY. PREPARE YOURSELF.*

"I have to go," I tell Nicki. "My agent's coming for you—really. She's outside. But I can't . . . I just . . ." My lungs can't fill with enough air. A hive of trouble outside, all waiting to pluck at me, dissect me, shove microphones in my face, asking the same questions over and over again: "Where's Fielding? Is it true? What will happen to Jenna and Jonah?"

As though I know any of the answers.

6

SECRET AGENT MAN

FIELDING

My James Bond act is the dumbest thing I have ever thought of. Which makes it kind of weird that it works. I know I'm supposed to be mad—my world is collapsing and all that stuff—but I'm having a hell of a time.

Before we even got out of the restaurant, I was on the phone with my parents, explaining to Mom that, no, I'm not gay, I just have gay friends, which I guess to them had as much credibility as the old "I didn't, but some other people at the party did" excuse, because Dad chimed in with "Son, I knew it at your first talent show. We'll always love you no matter what." I guess it was a mistake for me to sing "Somewhere Over the Rainbow," but—what the hell—I was seven years old.

"Charlie!" some photographer yelled. "How's it feel to be the beard?"

Charlie responded by kissing me deeply and passionlessly

and squeezing a part of me she normally doesn't have access to as though it was the cliff she was clinging to for dear life. Or dear career, anyway.

We parted, and I went home, having to go through a phalanx—power SAT word number forty-two!—of photographers to get into my house. The phone was ringing non-stop. I took the first seven calls from Jo, but I ended up just turning the phone off after she told me I had to make personal calls to the fan club presidents in twelve countries telling them that the rumors are false.

I went to bed instead.

And then I got up and looked out my window. Phalanx. Swarm. Mob. Turned on my phone—twenty-five new voice mails, a hundred text messages. I didn't check them.

I did call James, though. "Hey," I said. "How are you doing?"

"I feel great," he said. "Do you have any idea how freaking fantastic it feels to not have to live a lie anymore?"

I sighed. Nope. I told James I'd call him later.

I needed a pick-me-up, so I called Jo and set my plan in motion. One of Jo's assistants, Ryan, drove over to my house with a box. He then left in my car, and the jackals followed him.

I emerged fifteen minutes later in a Dodgers cap and the maintenance uniform I had Ryan bring over. It's five miles to the studio from my apartment and, this being Southern California, it's a beautiful day—seventy-six degrees and sunny. I had a great bike ride and got all the way to the studio door unnoticed. I pressed my key card against the security pad, and I was in. And still invisible.

I enjoyed being invisible so much that I kept it up, walking past all my coworkers without even getting glanced at. I have to say it was really nice.

So here I am, next to the studio door with Charlie and The Contest Winner, whose name I don't know and who is too young for me and who will most likely hate me when she finds out that I'm secretly gay and my romance with Charlie is a lie. Or that I'm not secretly gay but everything with Charlie is untrue.

"Excuse me, miss," I say to The Contest Winner. "Are you sure your tour's complete?"

"Oh, yeah, thanks," she says, then looks under the Dodgers cap. "Oh. My. GOD! Jo— Fielding!"

I put my finger up to my lips. "Yeah, I'm kind of going incognito here," I say, smiling. I look at Charlie. She's looking terrified of the sounds of the hungry sharks outside the door. "What's up, sweetie?" I say to Charlie and plant a big kiss on her just because I'm pretty sure she'll be horrified at the idea of kissing a maintenance guy.

"Oh my God, you guys are so cute," The Contest Winner says. "I just hope I can find a relationship like yours one day."

"Careful what you wish for," Charlie says into my ear. I smile at her—a genuine smile. We've got our misery in common, anyway.

"So," I say to The Contest Winner, "we're going to do a Great Escape number here. Do you wanna come?"

"You mean . . . I mean, well, the studio has a car taking me back to my hotel."

"Cool. Where you staying?"

"Disneyland Grand Californian. We added a few days on to the trip because my little brother really wanted to go to Disneyland, and since, like, when are we ever going to be in Southern California again, well—"

"Anaheim. Awesome. It's perfect. Like really, completely, totally perfect."

"Field, honey," Charlie says, smiling. "What are you talking about?"

"Well, Charlie dear," I say and lean closer to her, "I know you were busy escorting— I'm sorry, what's your name?"

"Nicki Kenny."

"—Nicki around, but today's shooting has been canceled. I think the network execs have a major case of mad about the fake script. Or possibly a case of 'Oh my God, Fielding is gay!'–itis."

"You're gay?" Nicki says.

"No, I just—"

"That's cool. My cousin's gay. We go to high school together. He's in drama, too. You guys would probably be cute together. So, like, the hugging and kissing and stuff, that's just like a cover because you're afraid America won't accept the real you?"

51

"That's it, pretty much," I say. Charlie is grinding her heel into my toe trying to get me to shut up, but now that I've tasted freedom, I'm not going back in my cage. "So, anyway, Nicki, Charlie and I have no work today and we're being stalked by evil paparazzi. So we're going to escape in disguise and maybe go hide at your hotel for a while. Does that sound okay?"

"Oh my God. That is like the most tragic thing I've ever heard. How you have to hide the real you. I mean, I totally get it, of course. But, yeah, of course I want to do the Great Escape. It sounds awesome! But are you guys, like—are you allowed at Disneyland?"

Everybody knows the Family Network doesn't like the Mouse. It's not in our contracts or anything, but Charlie and I know very well we're not to be photographed on Disney property, seeing one of their movies, or pretty much acknowledging the existence of the Mouse in any way. Which means nobody will be looking for us at one of their hotels.

"No," Charlie says. "We are not." She's giving me the look of death I've grown so familiar with.

"Yeah, sure we are," I say.

"No," she says. "We're not." And then she stops pretending to be nice in front of our guest. Nicki's going to have a hell of a story for her blog. "Dammit, Fielding, we are not going to go set foot on Disney property! We may as well announce that we don't want to work anymore! We may as well just tear up our contracts, and maybe you're that irresponsible, but I was born into this business and I know how it works and what you do and what you simply don't do. And one of the things you simply don't do is infuriate your employer at a delicate time! Call Jo and ask her!"

"Yeah, I'm kind of not taking her calls right now." I turn to Nicki. "I'm really sorry. Looks like we won't be able to escape to the Magic Kingdom after all. Do you know where Candi's office is? The producer who, unless I miss my guess, escorted you in here?"

"Down the hall to the left?"

"Yeah. Go tell her you're ready for the car to the hotel. And have a great time at Disneyland."

"Thanks!" I kiss her on the cheek—since I'm gay now, I can do something like that without it seeming creepy—and send her blushing down the hall.

As soon as she's out of sight, Charlie turns on me. " 'Unless I miss my guess'? Is there another seventeen-year-old in America who says stuff like that?"

"Hey, baby, I told you I'm not like the other guys." I flash my best charming grin, the one I use at all the teen magazine photo shoots.

Charlie hits me on the arm. Kind of hard.

"Ow!" I shout.

"Toughen up, Denise. Now we have to think. What the hell are we going to do? This is a crisis! We have to get out of sight! But there's nowhere for us to go!"

"Well. First you have to get a uniform. As much as it pains me to do this, I'm gonna have to call Jo."

"'*As much as it pains me*'? Is it, like, you being pretentious, or is it you being weird?"

"Do I have to choose? Can't I be pretentious *and* weird? And sex*ay*?"

"Yeah, listen. I don't care what that bimbo in the green bikini thought, but talking like that is definitely not sex*ay*."

So Charlie was searching Twitter for pictures of me. Purely for professional reasons, I guess. "Me call Jo now," I grunt, caveman style. "If can figure out how use phone. Girl always on phone. Maybe can help."

Charlie smiles. "It's actually an improvement."

I hit number one on my speed dial and Jo picks up before the phone even rings.

"Jesus, Fielding, you have to answer your phone sometimes. How am I supposed to manage a crisis if you're out of touch? This is really not helpful!"

"Okay. Um . . . thanks for the uniform and the car and stuff. I need another favor so we can get out of sight."

"Well, at least you're talking sense. You guys need to be completely off the radar for at least a week or until some drunken singer gets out of a limo with no underwear on, whichever comes first."

"So, early this afternoon?"

"Hilarious. What do you need?"

I tell her, and then add, "Uh, and we need a place to stay. Like, I don't know, somewhere out of the way where nobody's gonna look for us. But somewhere we can drive to, since we can't really go to an airport. It's not like we can check in to the Hotel Bel-Air and camp out."

There's a long silence. "Fielding, remember where half your money is?"

"In your fleet of Lexuses?"

"Funny," she deadpans. "No, real estate." I hear tapping on a keyboard. "Okay. How does a beach house in Carpinteria sound? You've owned it for a year, and it's currently without tenants. My notes here say it needs some work."

"Who among us doesn't?"

"Great. Now you're a philosopher. I'll have Ryan bring keys. Call me when you get there and I'll keep you updated."

I have to give it to her. She delivers. Or, more accurately, one of her assistants, Ryan, delivers. Again. He shows up in about an hour—an hour we've spent cowering in the greenroom for *Stacey's Sorcery for Girls!*, another Family Network production, about a teen witch at a boarding school, and which the Family Network lawyers will tell you is nothing like any other show or series of books about teen wizards.

"Hey, Fielding," Ryan says.

"Ryan," I say. " 'Sup."

"Thanks for getting me out of the office. She's a complete nightmare today."

"I can only imagine. Sorry about that."

"Eh, I knew what I was signing up for. Here are your keys, here's Charlie's uniform, and the van is outside."

"Great. I'll get Candi to call a car to get you back to the office," I tell him.

"No worries. I packed my bike in the back of the van."

"It'll take you an hour and a half to bike back to your office!"

"Yeah, if I'm lucky," he says, smiling, and disappears.

"Here," I say, handing the uniform to Charlie.

She unfolds it, looks at it, and says, "No. No. Fielding, what if I get photographed in this?" Charlie twists her hair into some kind of knot and scratches her eyebrows, which she always does on camera and I'm only just now realizing maybe it's something she does normally.

"See, the whole idea is that nobody would ever look for you in this because they know you'd never wear it, so we can get out of here without being photographed."

Charlie glares at me and stalks off to her dressing room.

And half an hour later, we cruise right past the over-whelming paparazzi—all eighty-something of them—in our blue coveralls and climb into a bright yellow van with KOLODNY BROS. RUG SUCKERS—WE CLEAN YOUR CARPETS RIGHT! on the side.

Charlie pops her Bluetooth headset into her ear and talks nonstop to her agent about strategy, about what an idiot I am, about how she wants Martinka to handle the network, and about what an idiot I am. After about an hour, we make a pit stop. Well, I do, anyway. Charlie is afraid of gas station convenience store cameras recording her in coveralls, so she is doing her camel imitation, staying in the van. I make my way inside, use the bathroom, and buy us a couple of drinks—this being California, even the gas station convenience store has Purest Water for Charlie. Nobody notices me. The tabloids at the counter are several days old and still about some other celebrity couple, one of whom may have had a "Naughty Night with the Nanny!" Soon that'll be me and Charlie on the cover of all those tabloids.

Right now, though, I'm nobody. Just a guy in Rug Suckers coveralls.

I think I love being nobody.

I get back to the van, open the door, and say, "I'm nobody! Who are you? Are you nobody, too? Then there's a pair of us—don't tell! They'd banish us, you know."

Charlie leans over to her Bluetooth. "Hang on a sec," she says to her right cheek. "You're not the manliest guy on earth, but you're definitely not Emily Dickinson, and you're not nobody. You're a tool. No, not you," she reassures whoever she's on the phone with. "Fielding. Yeah." She returns to ignoring me and talks, her phone sitting on the van's center console.

I think about the prospect of listening to her talk about me for another hour the way she's doing now.

"Well, no, I don't *think* he's gay, but it doesn't really matter what I think. He's totally fine with that being the public perception. I know. Naive. No, you know, when you see him up close, he's not actually that cute. And definitely not careful enough with the personal grooming and hygiene to be gay."

Fortunately this Rug Suckers van is fully equipped. I grab the hose of the cordless shop vac behind the front seats and suck Charlie's phone right into an oblivion of dirt and pet hair.

"Hello?" she says. "Can you hear me? You're breaking up!" She grabs frantically for the phone on the center console, only to see me holding the Rug Sucker, which allows her to do the math.

She yells at me, using a string of expletives we are actually contractually forbidden from saying on Family Network property. I know she's angry, but I can't help smiling. America's sweetheart is calling me names that would make a truck driver blush.

"Well," I say, "I'm pretty sure what you've suggested is physically impossible, but should all the right equipment present itself, I'm not averse to giving it a try. Shall we go, then?"

"Great. So you've got a phone, you get contact with the outside world, and I'm like this prisoner in the nineteenth century. Since you talk like you live there anyway, that's probably not a big hardship for you, but it is for me. Really fair."

"Here," I say, handing her the Rug Sucker. I place my phone on the center console. "Fair and square."

Charlie gleefully sucks my phone into the shop vac, then turns it off and faces forward. "Somehow I thought that would be more satisfying," she says.

"Whoa, if I had a quarter for every time I've heard *that* . . . ," I say, and I see a smile trying to escape through her gritted teeth.

We spend the next forty-five minutes in complete, wonderful silence.

7

"LONG AND WINDING ROAD" REMIX

CHARLIE

Five thousand four hundred. That's how many seconds are in one and a half hours. I know because I've been doing mental math since we left the Family Network lot and got on the PCH to avoid any would-be followers from LA who would probably take the 101 up the coast to try and find us. But no one will find us because Fielding's real estate investment is tucked into the middle of nowhere. It's probably the longest we've ever been together and said nothing. Usually we have lines to run, dialogue to test out, or songs to learn. Or photo ops to figure out. But with none of that laid out for us, there's apparently nothing to say.

"I thought you said it was a house," I say to Fielding, who mouths the words to a song on the radio. He's perfected the lip sync after we both endured hours of brutal practice on set. And like it or not, his lips are pretty perfect, too. I try to avoid looking at them.

Fielding puts the van in park and shrugs, looking out the window. "Guess I was wrong."

We have no bags, no luggage handlers, no bellboy grinning ear to ear, no public fawning over us. "This is really weird, huh?" I take a few steps on the stone driveway and survey the area.

"Well, it's not exactly an ode to modernism," Fielding says as he looks to the left at the Tuscan-style farmhouse, "but it'll do."

It's one of his typically understated responses. We tentatively explore the grounds. Rather than a beach hut, Fielding is the proud owner of an old fruit plantation. Rows of trees, a canopy of vines between stone walls, all with dramatic ocean views of the Pacific smashing onto the boulders and cliffs below. Fielding takes it all in and I watch him without the ever-present spotlight: how funny he looks in his carpet-cleaning gear. He asks, "How bizarre is it that I own this place and have never seen it?"

"There's a lot that's fundamentally odd about this," I say, but I don't elaborate because I'm scared Fielding will think I'm superficial for worrying about our jobs, for focusing on what we've left behind, on what happens next. Or make fun of me for feeling slightly naked, a tortoise without its shell, naked for all the world to see. Not literally, of course—that's another prohibited activity per my contract—but exposed without the padding of personal assistants or crew or staff on hand to fulfill my every wish. I realize I don't even know when the last time I bought myself a soda was, or even water. Even Fielding bought my bottle of Purest today. How pathetic is it that I don't even know what it costs? And how nice is it that he knows me well enough to give me what I need?

As if reading my mind—which is possible given that we've worked fifteen-hour days, traveled to more than twenty countries, and basically spent every waking hour together for the past three-plus years—Fielding says, "Here's the thing: we can have tunnel vision, zooming in on all the issues at hand, which are sort of out of our control right now . . ."

"You sound like your agent talking," I tell him.

"Whatever. The point is, we don't really have control over stuff, so we can either worry about everything and freak out . . ."

"Or?" I ask, going down a few steps from the circular driveway and finding that the stairs lead to a sprawling orchard filled with fruit trees, the scent of citrus ripe and warm in the late afternoon sun.

Fielding bounds down the steps two or three at a time and leans in to smell one of the lemons on a tree. He tests the avocados, chucking one at me. "Or we can enjoy the fact that for once almost no one knows where we are, no one can lay claim to our time. It's like the ultimate vacation. And we've earned it."

In the fading sunlight, the rippling rays weaving through his hair, in the breathtaking beauty of this place, I feel my shoulders sag. What a relief. No interviews. No chasing. No expectations. Just us. I unzip my polyester-blend nightmare of an outfit, revealing the T-shirt and jeans I had on prior to covert operations. Maybe this won't be so bad.

"Even though we're stuck here with each other," Fielding adds. My stomach tightens.

"Leave it to you to ruin a perfectly fine moment." I storm off, inspecting the fruit as I go, holding on to the avocado as though it's someone's hand. Security in a vegetable. Or is it a fruit? Probably Fielding would know this since his dumbness was just a front. Probably he would know the complete history of the avocado and what its Latin name is and he'd make fun of me because I don't know any of that. I was too busy studying my expressions in the mirror growing up to learn Latin. Too busy ditching my money-sucking parents to memorize anything but lines and legal jargon.

The orchard is long, with row after row of untended trees, overgrown grass, and a bunch of fallen fruit littering the ground. I walk, letting my palms graze the tops of the grass stalks, still holding the avocado, until I leave many of the trees behind and stumble, nearly literally—I'm not the most graceful, despite hours logged in dance lessons—upon a sort of chapel. Surrounded by huge stones, the small outbuilding is made of smooth gray and white stone bricks; its roof, once tiled in red terra-cotta, is only half there. As the sun sinks lower over the distant water, I hoist myself up on the wall and sing softly.

Singing used to be an escape for me. In the shower, in the

car, as I was falling asleep. But once it became a job, like acting, I never enjoyed it as much. There's a constant inner critic worrying if I'm flat or pitchy or singing the wrong lyrics. But with only the fruit and rocks as my witness, I let the words out, singing the Beatles' song "The Long and Winding Road," and wonder where it will lead me next. I'm almost at the bridge, about to sing about being alone, when I realize I'm not.

"You know the actual long and winding road is in Scotland?" Fielding shouts, perched in one of the trees a few feet away.

I stay put on the wall, shouting back, "In fact, I did know that. It's the B842, if you're wondering, a road near Paul McCartney's farm."

Fielding hops down from the tree carrying something in his hands, and meets me halfway, stopping before he's actually at the wall. "So we both like the Beatles. Who'd have thought?"

I fight the urge to say that ninety-eight percent of human beings probably like that band, because maybe Fielding is trying to be kind. Or maybe he's just bored. "So what do we do now, O Guru of Knowledge?"

Fielding chucks the object in his hand at me. "Make lemonade?"

I manage to catch the thing and laugh. "This isn't a lemon, you dolt." I walk toward him, leaving the crumbling chapel behind. Fielding grins.

"I know that. It's an, um—an artichoke. Or something." He blushes. He hates being incorrect and often produces fake statistics to prove a point.

"Oh, so we don't know everything about everything now, do we?" I say and smell the fruit. "This not-lemon-not-artichoke is, in fact, a cherimoya." I wait to see if he'll contradict me. "Inside it's white. It's delicious." We stand there facing each other, with no script, and silence pulses through us. The breeze picks up, and right when I think Fielding will kill the moment with information about agriculture or make some comment about my tan rubbing off (which it is since I missed my spray appointment this afternoon), he points to the avocado and cherimoya.

"I'm incredibly hungry."

The ocean glimmers in front of us, and the house we've yet to explore beckons us inside. "Me, too! We sort of forgot to eat today."

"Maybe we can rustle up some sort of late afternoon grub?" He gets an idea and sprints away, leaving me with the fruit.

I pick a couple of oranges and a lime, and follow him to the back of the house. Underneath a trellis of vines, Fielding finds a garden that bulges with produce, even though much of it is rotten or forgotten. Staked tomato plants climb skyward; overgrown patches of herbs and a multitude of flowers all mingle together.

"Check it out—a forgotten garden," Fielding says, still in

his carpet-cleaning costume. He kneels down, picking through weeds to unearth a zucchini. "I'm thinking we might just have the makings for a salad." He gathers some vegetables into his arms and we walk together back toward the van, which looks ridiculous and clashes horribly with the serene surroundings.

Again, we're not used to the lack of dialogue, and it takes me a bit to get the feel for talking freely. "The cherimoya is also known as the custard apple. It kind of has a sherbet texture."

Fielding nods as he pulls the key from his pocket and unlocks the arched wooden front door. "How come you know so much about fruit?"

I walk inside, my skin immediately chilled by the dark of the house. The walls are thick and the warm outside air hasn't filtered in. The entryway is like a tunnel, and we follow it into an enormous main room. "My grandma cooked a ton," I explain. "When I first started this whole thing—doing the commercials for Twinkle Toes . . ." I walk through the great room, admiring the wide wooden beams on the high ceilings, the enormous fireplace with its marble mantel.

"Twinkle Toes, for your own little princess!" Fielding quotes. "I totally remember those ads. They were on every two seconds." He shakes his head. "It's funny to think that you were that kid—the one who had to walk on tiptoes and smile in that oversized crown. My sister used to want to be you."

From the recesses of my memory, I pull the theme music and hum it. "You know, those shoes sucked. They pinched my toes. I have an actual scar from them. Seriously."

At the other end of the great room is another arched doorway. "Come here," Fielding commands, and I hear the plunk of the vegetables being dropped onto a wood table. I walk in and rescue the biggest tomato before Fielding brings it to an untimely death by dropping. "Welcome to my kitchen—to both of us, I guess."

"This is great! It's sort of half antique, half modern." I run around, searching the open shelves for bowls, a pan— any items previous tenants left behind that we can scrounge up for our impromptu feast. I love old houses, places with histories that really mean something, tell stories, rather than just simple cardboard backdrops of Paris or Ye Olde Candy Shoppe. It's not very Hollywood of me, but I like a little dirt around the edges, some character.

"Oh, the cutting boards! They're original. Look how old they are, all those marks . . ." I can't contain my excitement at a real kitchen, one that could produce actual food rather than just being for show. When they feature food on *Jenna & Jonah*, either it's made out of carefully sculpted clay that's hand-painted but still wouldn't fool a toddler or else they have real food, like a cheeseburger, but it's cold and painted, too, so the bright colors show up better on camera and any steam that wafts from a fakely freshly baked cookie is really smoke from a little blower machine. Seeing it all up close pretty much ruins television ads for restaurants, because you see the bullshit that is the industry—all that visual pull for something you can't even sink your teeth into.

"See," I say to Fielding, "Grandma Ruth always had flowers everywhere, and food—too much to eat in one sitting. So we'd sort of make all this stuff together—homemade jams, and breads . . ." As I talk, Fielding washes the vegetables and I begin to slice open the avocado. "Even guacamole. Can you get the oven going?"

"Sure," he says. His eyebrows are raised as I remove the avocado's stone with one solid clunk of a knife.

"What?" I put the thing down, wiping my face with my hands, checking my hair for bird droppings or something. "Do I have something on me?"

Fielding shakes his head and hands me a cookie sheet. "No . . . it's just . . . I've never really seen you . . ." He pauses, and I wonder if this is it. He hasn't really seen me. And maybe I haven't really seen him. "I've never seen you cook before." I wait for him to say more, but he doesn't.

"Well, you've also never eaten anything I've made before, so watch out!" I threaten with the zucchini in hand.

He wields a summer squash and we have a vegetable duel until the zucchini breaks and we go back to cooking.

"The oven-roasted tomatoes will be perfect later," I say as I slide the tray in the oven.

"Like how much later?" He clutches his stomach.

I feel the stove. "Well, um, a lot longer than I thought if we can't get this thing to heat up. I thought you turned it on?"

"I did," he insists. "Hold on. Let me check the pilot light." He fiddles with a few things, switches a knob, and suddenly the heat flows. "See? All set."

"The consummate handyman. Thanks."

While our late lunch cooks, we give ourselves a tour of the rest of the house.

Fielding says, "Six bedrooms, three baths—not bad for a boy from—what do you like to say?—the armpit of the Midwest?"

Away from the show's hustle and the glare of paparazzi, my quick summary of Fielding's roots sounds mean. "I do say that, don't I?" My voice is small, apologetic.

"You do, but that's just because you've never been."

Fielding heads up the stone staircase, follows it as it curves around into a master suite that would be perfect if it weren't filled with floor-to-ceiling boxes and furniture covered with tarps.

"Where are we supposed to sleep?" I ask.

Fielding reverts right back to his on-set persona and echoes Jonah's ever-earnest voice. "Gee, Jenna, I thought you'd sort it out for us!"

Just hearing the change in his tone sets off my professional buttons, and instead of asking him more about Cincinnati or anything else in his background, I shoot right back with my optimistic Jenna voice. "Of course, Jonah! You can depend on me to get the job done! Together, we'll sort it out!" I spit this last part out before I bolt down the stairs to check on the tomatoes.

8

WHO ARE YOU?

AARON-FIELDING

I really feel like I could stay here forever. The sea, the fresh fruit and vegetables . . . All I really need is the right person to share it with.

Sadly, that person is not the person who is here right now. I don't think.

I slept for twelve hours the first night, then went into town and picked up some supplies—cereal, soy milk, and a big enough stack of books to keep me reading for at least a week. We're miles from the nearest place to buy a TV and video games, which is probably just as well—I kind of like being unplugged.

Well, almost unplugged. I dug into the Rug Sucker machine and retrieved my phone. I could have gotten Charlie's out, too, but then I would have had to listen to her on the phone constantly, and it would have stressed me out. Probably I'm a terrible person.

But I did want to talk to Mom and Dad, just so they wouldn't worry about me being missing.

"Hello, sweetie," Mom says. "How are you doing? Where are you, anyway?" I hear a lot of noise in the background.

"I'm hiding out at a beach house. Where are you?"

"At a gymnastics meet, of course. Where else would I be?" I feel this little pang—Mom has moved on from being my stage mom to being my sister's gymnastics mom because I'm supposed to be all grown up, or close enough to pass.

"I don't know. How's everybody taking the news of my alleged gayness?"

"Honestly, honey, nobody's that surprised." I could tell Mom to insist on my heterosexuality to everyone, but that would look desperate, and, anyway, I don't really care.

"So what else is going on at—?"

"Listen, honey, I've gotta go. They're calling your sister's group to the beam. Call me soon—love you!"

"I love you, too," I say, but I don't know if she's listening or not.

When I get back to the house, Charlie starts in on me as soon as I get in the door. "You know, you have to leave me a note when you leave the house. I swear to God, if you leave me stuck here, I'll hunt you down wherever you are and—" More colorful, expletive-laden details follow.

"Why would I leave you stuck here?" I ask as I put the grocery bags down on the counter.

"Because you hate me! Because you know I'm in hell here—no phone, no Internet, completely isolated from the outside world. And my only way out would be to walk into town and hang around waiting for a ride and get recognized and get photographed in clothes that cause me to *play against type*, which is not what I need right now, okay?"

"Chuck," I say, which is probably a mistake, because she hates that. "I don't hate you. I mean, you know that, right? It's not like you don't get on my nerves, but I really don't hate you."

"And yet here you are calling me Chuck, which you know I hate. So if you don't hate me, why are you being such a dick to me?"

She makes a good point. I rake my hands through my product-free hair. "I dunno. I think it's like a bad habit or something."

"Well, maybe you should take up smoking or something," Charlie says, "because you being a dick is getting kind of old."

I busy myself putting groceries away. "You know as well as I do that smoking is specifically prohibited by our contract. I think that's paragraph twelve."

"Okay, then how about you pick your nose? I mean, that's a bad habit." Charlie sees the bag of kiwi fruit I've just pulled out and grabs one. "Love these, by the way."

"I know," I say. Her dressing room hasn't been without kiwi fruit as long as I've known her. "But the thing about nose

73

picking is, I mean, what do you do with the boogers? Because I can't, like, wipe them on my pants, and the flick is such a high-risk maneuver. You never know if it's going to go where you want it to go or just stay on the end of your finger—"

"I always just drop mine into my costar's lattes," Charlie says, smiling now for real.

"Hey! You told me that was a flavor shot!"

We both start laughing, and I put the rest of the groceries away.

"You know who bought the groceries today with the credit card with his own name on it?" I say after a minute. "Aaron Littleton, that's who."

"Who the hell is Aaron Littleton?" Charlie asks.

"He's me. Or, anyway, he's who I used to be. He's who I think I'm going to be again. I was thirteen when Mom picked my stage name, and I hate it. Fielding. I mean, it's not a name. It's a verb. Fielding. My name is a gerund. It's what American League designated hitters don't get to do."

A strange expression flits across Charlie's face, but it quickly goes away, replaced by the angry face she's had on pretty much ever since we got here. "Well, great, *Aaron*, I'm really glad you're finding yourself. But, you know, I already knew who I was, and despite the fact that I had to hang out with you, I liked who I was. Now I'm nobody."

"There's a pair of us," I say, trying to recapture what I thought was the relaxed good feeling between us that has somehow just evaporated.

"Emily Dickinson? Really? Do you want to shut yourself up in your house for, like, a decade? Actually, you know what? You probably do. But I don't. And you haven't given me a choice. God, you are so selfish!" she yells at me and stomps up the stairs. I stare at the empty staircase for a minute. I understand why she storms away when I say something mean, but right now I really have no idea what I did. Maybe she accused me of hating her because she actually hates me.

I write a note and put it on the table: "I'm taking a book down to the beach to read. I would not abandon you here. But if you want to leave, here are the keys." I place the keys to the Kolodny Brothers Rug Suckers van atop the note and take a book down to the beach.

It's a really good book. It's a mystery about a private eye who's hired to solve a case he's not really supposed to solve. He gets pushed around by a variety of powerful people, only a pawn in their game. I identify.

Hours pass, and I head inside and find the note and the keys gone. I'm not really surprised. She probably wants to play the clueless girlfriend wronged by my deception. I think she'll be able to sell that—I snuck around behind her back, she never knew about my secret life . . . She can go on some daytime talk show and cry about how I made a fool of her. It's a pretty good idea. Well, good for her.

I spend some time wandering around the house. The paint is peeling. The floor under the first-floor toilet is sagging. Somebody's probably going to crash through there into the basement while they're on the can. I hope it's not me. Though it does mean a trip to the bathroom is riskier and more exciting than usual. I might even say "extreme."

"I'm Fielding Withers," I say in my best sports announcer voice, "and welcome to X-treme crapping!"

"Well," Charlie's voice says, "I see I'm not the only one who gets bored around here."

I emerge from the bathroom and find Charlie standing there. This is surprising enough. What's doubly surprising is that she is dressed in the Rug Suckers coveralls and holding a can of paint in one hand and a big paper bag that says CARPINTERIA HARDWARE in the other.

"Anyway, I thought you were Aaron now," she says.

"Uh. Yeah. I, uh—I thought you were going to go on some TV show and cry about how I'd deceived you."

Charlie places her bags on the floor and begins pulling out painting supplies—a roller, a pan, and a plastic drop cloth emerge one by one.

"You think I'd throw you under the bus like that just to save my career?" she finally replies.

"Well. I mean, it'd kind of be the smart move."

Charlie sighs. "You really need to read the celebrity magazines more often. In light of the fake script thing, it would be hard for me to say I'm in on one deception and not on the other. Me as the victim is going to be a tough sell since I was *alone* at the farmer's market with the fake script."

"I would say I'm sorry, but that would be insincere."

"Oh, I know. And you're so real, so small-town—or should I say so Littleton, so above the petty deceptions of us morally bankrupt Hollywood types."

"Littleton! Like it! Okay, I'll give you points for the name thing, but, you know, we really need to get this straight. Cincinnati is not Los Angeles, but it's not a small town. It's a major Midwestern city with a population of over three hundred thousand. So whenever you're getting snotty about how I'm morally superior because of my small-town roots, let's just be clear and say that I am so real, so small-*city*. Four years of this crap. You know how many millions of people don't live on either coast?"

"You've obviously forgotten our concert tour of the CD departments of various Valu-Marts in the Midwest and South."

"Oh, yeah. That was kind of fun!"

Charlie spends a long moment looking at me, then picks up her paint cans. "Yeah. Like dental surgery is kind of fun. Whatever. I spent the morning measuring rooms—did you know a dollar bill is six inches long? Makes a handy little ruler in a pinch—and I'm going to paint this afternoon."

"You're going to paint."

"Yes!" she says, grabbing her stuff and heading up the stairs. "I may be stuck in the middle of nowhere, but I'm not going to sleep in a room with peeling paint."

"What have you ever painted before?" I yell up the stairs to her.

"How hard could it possibly be?" she yells back. And then she's gone.

I don't see her again until dinner, which I cook.

"I'm going for a run," she announces when she comes downstairs. "I'll just grab something later."

I look at my vegetable stew and couscous. It's colorful, and yet it looks kind of sad now. I eat it while reading.

Charlie returns from her run before dark, takes a long shower, and roots around in the kitchen, apparently not interested in eating my couscous. Her loss. It was pretty good, even if I didn't have enough cayenne to make a decent hot sauce.

The next morning, I am awakened by stomping sounds. I stagger out into the hallway, and there is Charlie, looking fit and sweaty and cute as hell with her ponytail and other interesting parts bobbing up and down as she runs up and down the stairs.

"What the hell are you doing?" I croak out.

"I'm running the stairs!" she says.

"Yeah. Why?"

She pauses, jogging in place. With great effort, I focus on her eyes, which are not bouncing up and down. "Listen Fiel— *Aaron*. If that is your name. I'm not like you. I can't do nothing all day. I can't do nothing pretty much ever. I have to keep busy or I go insane. I've been on the go since I was two. And I have to exercise on the small chance that anyone ever wants to photograph me in a bikini again. So I'm running the stairs. Good for the glutes."

And down she goes.

We give each other space for the next day or two. I'm kind of afraid I'm going to say something that sets her off again, and she is, I guess, still mad at me. I read more than one book per day, I take naps, I ignore the trades, Perez Hilton, and TMZ, and I don't care about any of it.

Charlie keeps busy, painting three rooms. After the first two, she figured out that she should put tape on the ceiling to avoid getting paint on it when she paints the walls. Even with splotches of paint on the ceiling, though, the rooms are very much improved. She's picked colors that are bright and vibrant, which fits her personality—well, the vibrant part anyway—and the rooms she's painted look warm, inviting, and fun.

On the evening of the third day, she graces me with her presence at dinner, a pasta dish I've made with garden vegetables and a can of chickpeas I got at the store in town. Tentatively, she takes a bite. "Whoa. This is really good," she says.

"Thanks," I say. "Hey, the rooms look great, by the way. You've really warmed up the place."

"Thank you," she says. We don't say anything for a minute, but it doesn't seem like she's thinking angry, resentful thoughts; she's just eating in silence.

Well, I'm not thinking angry, resentful thoughts, and I actually have no idea what Charlie is thinking. What I eventually start thinking is that I wouldn't mind doing this for a while. With Charlie, I mean. It's nice to be alone, but it's also nice to be able to talk to another human being once in a while. There's something comforting about the knowledge that someone else is doing something in the house. Maybe I like Charlie better when I don't have to see her all the time. Is that mean? I could probably say the same thing for just about anybody—certainly my parents.

"You know," I say, "this is really nice."

"Yeah," Charlie says.

"The rooms look great, by the way."

"You said that already, genius."

Did I? She's got me off balance. "Well. I see. In that case, they're hideous."

"Thank you! I mean, if you actually like the paint job, it pretty much defeats the whole point!"

She looks mischievous. It's kind of adorable.

"So, you spent three days painting just to piss me off?"

"Well, not *just* to piss you off, no. But I was kind of hoping it would have that effect."

"You don't like your landlord? I mean, you gotta admit, the rent is *very* reasonable."

Charlie smiles and puts both hands behind her head. She appears to be adjusting her ponytail, but she's also drawing attention to her world-famous assets. "I guess. The place is kind of a dump, though."

"Well, what do you want for nothing? I happen to think

the landlord is a helluva guy. Charming, intelligent, good-looking, and an amazing dancer."

The sun is dipping into the ocean outside, and the light in here gets dim and yellow. And Charlie really is beautiful. "Yeah. Too bad he's gay," Charlie says, flashing a devilish grin at me.

"What if he wasn't?" I ask. The question hangs there, and for once in her life, Charlie doesn't seem to have anything to say.

She just smiles. And finally she says, "I'll do the dishes. Thanks for cooking."

"Um. Anytime!"

I go up to bed but find it very hard to sleep. What the hell just happened down there? Or did anything at all happen? Would I be a complete idiot if something happened? Would I be a complete idiot if nothing happened?

★9★

LIVING WITH YOU, LIVING WITHOUT YOU

CHARLIE

"You know what we need, Field—I mean, Aaron?" I say as he busies himself slicing tomatoes. I can't get used to calling him Aaron, but now Fielding sounds fake, too. He looks up but doesn't respond with any words, as though he wants me to pay him for any dialogue. "A montage." He raises his eyebrows, hair falling over his forehead in his trademark way. I want to brush it away and touch his stubbled face—until he gives me a look that suggests I'm an idiot. Then I want to chop all his hair off in his sleep. "You know how they'd make almost a whole episode of flashbacks? That time we recorded 'Living with You, Living without You,' when you—"

"Jonah—"

"Right, when Jonah had appendicitis? It was, like, no new footage, just a few minutes of us in that lame hospital room—"

Aaron finally breaks into a grin. "So ridiculous—it was

the same room they used for global studies, just with a gurney and fake medical devices beeping." We lock eyes, laughing, remembering.

"Anyway, that's sort of what we need now, a montage with music over it—we'd get the house all repaired . . ."

Aaron joins in. "Yeah, with me yanking weeds and planting new trees . . ."

I let myself get excited, my voice rises in pitch, and my hands flail. "Then, just as the grounds are looking great, our careers would get a makeover, too. We'd remember who we used to be before and we'd suddenly be back on top of the teen world, but we wouldn't have had to deal with this part."

"And what part is that, exactly?" Aaron puts the tomatoes on a cookie sheet and drizzles olive oil on top.

I bite my lip. "The stuff in between. The hard stuff. The crap. That's why they don't show it in movies and TV, because it's impossible to document."

Aaron slides the baking sheet into the oven and comes over to me. For a second I think he's about to hug me, reach for me. But instead he puts his hand on my shoulder in one gesture of pity. "That hard part is called life. Reality. And it's what you don't know how to deal with."

Feeling deflated like the withered helium balloons on our prom set, I leave the main house where Aaron and his starkness rebuff me and head outside. The property is amazing, in need of major repairs—like, say, paint, plastering, and a toilet that flushes—but it is a thing of beauty. Just like that old cliché of something beautiful hiding under the messy exterior. Off the kitchen is a small patio, emptied of furniture but rimmed with more flowers, ones so tall they nearly bend over with their own weight. I study the blue, pink, and yellow bursts and then notice something way off to the left, halfway down the cliff side, nearly jumping off the ledge into the ocean. Across the uneven grass and along the rocky paths that haven't been tended in who knows how long, I walk toward what appears to be a small cabin. I lift a latch on the broken wooden gate and slip through, hoping the cabin also technically belongs to Aaron so I'm not trespassing and doomed to wind up in the tabloids for this embarrassment, too.

Inside, there's just one main room, with a double bed flanked by side tables made from old fruit crates, two oil lamps, a little bathroom with a claw-foot tub, and a view of the ocean from every square foot. In a word, it's perfect. I sit on the bed and feel, really for the first time in ages, my whole body. Tired. Hungry. The worry of what lurks in the rest of the world feels farther and farther away, and I lie back, wondering how I could have lasted so long playing the love-interest-next-door of someone who so clearly despises me. How could anyone have bought the whole charade?

Sure enough, when I wake up after my unexpected nap, the sky has darkened and I can only barely find my way back to the main house and Jonah—I mean Fielding—I mean

Aaron—is nowhere to be found. I try not to get creeped out to the point of calling the police, because the last thing I want is more scandal. First, I walk around from room to room, yelling "Fielding! Aaron!" and then "Jonah?" just to piss him off and because every so often I seriously do slip up, but when it's clear he's either hiding or been abducted or simply deserted me, I get back to what I know how to do.

I cook. I slice. I mash. I take the now perfectly oven-dried tomatoes out and combine a few of them with the ripe avocado, add some salt, some freshly squeezed lemon juice, some cayenne from the pantry, and produce a guacamole worthy of my grandma. The custard apple I scoop out and put into a simple blue bowl. Orange wedges complete my vegetarian paradise. The sun sets fully, leaving traces of red in the sky, and I light some candles, making the table look nice even though I'm alone.

It's not bad, really. The solitude. I'm just about to take my first bite of guacamole when a clatter jolts me. I grab a spreading knife as though I can butter an intruder to death.

"Relax, it's only me," Aaron announces, his arms full with brown bags, an old fishing cap pulled far down over his eyes. "Tell me you weren't starting without me."

I roll my eyes even though in the dim light the gesture might be wasted. "Thanks for leaving me in this run-down nightmare with no way of escaping and no idea where you'd gone."

Aaron lugs the bags over to the table, disrupting my

pretty display of plates and food. He looks at me, semi-disgusted, and says nothing. The worst punishment of all. Once, when I made a scene on set about the new cleaning fluid that made my wrists swell and hives appear on my back, he accused me of being a high-maintenance poodle and refused to speak to me for a whole week, except for our lines. So when he storms off, it's not a surprise, but it stings nonetheless. I sit for a second, then peer into the bags.

Fresh bread—not from a supermarket, but crusty, from a bakery, like I always order in delis even though I don't often get to eat it. Baby romaine lettuce. Fresh fish wrapped in brown paper. Coffee. Milk. A flashlight. My heart sinks. He hadn't left me; he had left me to get groceries, supplies. I put everything away, prep some more, and go find him.

He's not in the great room, not upstairs investigating the box-cluttered rooms, not outside in the orchard. I take the flashlight and go down to the little cabin and find him sitting on the front steps.

I stand there, about to apologize, when he breaks the growing silence. "Remember Season Two? That side plot when Mr. Connolly had to sing some song about taking a trip somewhere he'd never been?"

I nod. "Holiday Far Away." I think he ended up holidaying in New Jersey or somewhere equally exotic, but the song was a hit in the United States, perfectly timed for the holiday season here and guaranteed to become a holiday classic.

"Right. Well, that's sort of what I want to do. Here."

He looks up, and for just a second we are just two people. Two people near the ocean. Two people who don't really know each other at all.

"Thanks for the supplies," I say. "I have the fish cooking as we speak."

Aaron stands up. "And you'll actually eat?" I nod. "Bread, too?" Another nod from me.

"It'll be ready in ten minutes—fish doesn't take long." I stare at the ocean and then back at the little cabin.

"Long enough for me to get cleaned up," he says and disappears into the cabin. While he showers, I head back up to the kitchen and feel just the tiniest bit of excitement. This is the first meal I've made in a long time. The first one I've ever made for Fielding—Aaron—unless you count the time I threw a Hostess cupcake at his head in Taiwan and told him to get the hell up for an interview.

Aaron arrives, hair wet enough that it drips a little down his back, wetting his T-shirt, his eyes alive in the candlelight. He hands me another brown bag. "Look inside."

Our eyes meet as I try to thank him for the new clothes. "I don't know what to say."

"How about, thanks and let's hope they fit?" He glances around the kitchen. "Man, you put on a nice spread. You expecting company?"

"Just you," I say and point to the table, where the fish, poached in an orange-tarragon sauce, waits with slices of thick bread, cheeses Aaron picked up in town, and water I've flavored with hibiscus and sugar. I want to have him taste the sweetness, know it came from me, that I made it and not some caterer.

Aaron and I eat and he nods appreciatively. "Remind me to thank your grandma."

"You can't," I tell him, my voice solemn. "She died two years ago."

He pauses, waiting, and then I laugh.

"Just kidding," I say. And he's breathless with relief, his hand over his heart.

"God, I felt so bad," he says. "That's a sick joke."

"Actually," I say, all serous again, "it's true. She had pancreatic cancer. Diagnosed in September, gone four months later."

Aaron's face falls from grin to grimace. "Geez, Charlie. Now I feel horrible." Then he pauses. "Wait. You're screwing with me again, right? She didn't die. You're making it up." I lean forward so he can see my eyes. The candlelight will probably distort the brown lens color, making them amber and odd. "Oh, no. You're serious." I nod. He groans, reaching for my arm but then pulling back before making actual contact. "Hey, you really can act."

I chew a piece of bread and consider. "I can act. I just don't get the chance that often. And don't feel bad. Grandma Ruth would have laughed, too. She was that kind of lady."

"Did she teach you to make this fish?" Aaron finishes everything on his plate and clears it, running the water so it soaks in the oversized sink.

"No. That I made up just now. I mean, you had the tarragon outside and the oranges, so . . ." I wipe the table clean.

"I'm impressed." Aaron hands me the brown bag again. "Aren't you going to try them on at least?"

I peer into the bag. Who knows what shape, size, garment. My stomach churns when I picture Aaron picking a shirt out for me. Or a dress. It's intimate, choosing things for people. And we've never, in all our scenes or tours, exchanged gifts. Not that this is a gift. It's just an errand, right? My heart thuds in my chest.

"Playing against type," Aaron says. "That's good for you. You know, you're usually cast like Jenna, right? Even in commercials, you're all smiles and sort of neutered."

"Neutered?" I ask. "Like a cat?"

Aaron cracks up. I love being able to make him laugh. "No, not like as in surgically, but like with Jenna. She's a very safe character. She's the sort of girl who's so sweet that she's . . . impenetrable." He grins. "In more way than one." I open my mouth to object to his adolescent humor when he continues. "Jenna can barely manage sarcasm. Which is why, when you joke about a dead grandma, for example, it comes out of left field and I buy it."

"And Jonah's this all-American suck-up . . ." I take a bite of guacamole. "So if you're playing against type, you should be some thieving, conniving kid from the wrong side of the tracks, right?"

"Pretty much." Aaron nods. "And that's probably what I

would've been if I hadn't been in the right place at the right time all those years ago."

"Meaning?"

"Meaning, kids from Cincinnati don't have two-hundred-dollar sneakers." He holds up his foot. "They don't read Sartre or travel internationally and learn the other name for custard apple."

"Cherimoya."

"Exactly."

"But you know tons," I say. "You're always quoting Howard Zinn and Walt Whitman."

Aaron looks amused. "Well, I mean, I do hear America singing." He tilts his head, studying me. "You remembered?"

"Who could forget being called a"—I put on his mean voice—"total and complete ignoramus with little or no knowledge of the outside world, not to mention historic events, who ought to read some Howard Zinn or Walt Whitman to get a sense of the country that mysteriously loves you so much."

Aaron runs his hands through his hair. Without the work of the makeup trailer and the twelve products normally in it, or the tufts falling over his forehead that give him a softer appearance. "God, I did say that, didn't I? What an asshole I can be."

"Well, it worked. I mean, I ordered *A People's History of the United States* from Amazon."

"Did you read it?" Aaron asks, his eyes wide.

"Cover to cover," I say, deadpan. He's about to buy it when I punch his shoulder, only so it's a friendly gesture, nothing he could interpret as more than friendly—even if part of me feels like squeezing his hand. I shove the instinct away. "When would I have had time to crack that sucker? It's like twelve thousand pages."

"But did you check out the pictures?" he jokes, and I smirk back.

We go outside and find a place to sit in the dark orchard, talking as the moon rises until I don't know how much time has passed.

"How long do you think we have until we're discovered?" I ask.

Aaron props himself up on his arm, his legs stretched out in front of him. "A day? Twelve? Who knows?"

I stand up. "So it's just you and me for who knows how long?"

"Think you can handle the lack of makeup, the deafening sound of no audience?" he asks, only partially joking.

"I can handle more than you think," I tell him and glance over. His eyes are glued to mine and I have to look away, my breathing faster. "I've been dealing with auditions and rejections for longer than you've been out of diapers."

Aaron rises and moves to be close to me. We're closer than we have been since our last fake kiss, which I realize now is still a kiss, even if the motives weren't true. We lock eyes. In his eyes I see all the seasons of songs, of insults flung back and forth, and all the lies that led us to tonight. Without anyone to end the scene, to break for lunch, to say, "It's a wrap," we just keep going. Close enough that I can feel his warm breath in the cooling air. I wrap my arms around myself and say, just to be safer, just in case I think one thing and he thinks something else and I wind up humiliated, "I think I'm going to go get clean."

I grab the brown bag and jog away. Away from him and away from any temptation and confusion. The main house is too big, too boxed up, so I go to the cabin and fill the tub with hot water. Sinking into it, I let my hair out of its knot. With no brush and no flatiron, it will revert to its wavy nature. Realizing I can, I remove my contacts and scrub my skin clean of ForeverTan, which takes more effort than you might think. And when I stand up, I feel clean. Cleaner than ever, really. Then I remember I'm naked with nothing but dirty clothes or a carpet cleaner outfit to wear unless I look in the bag Aaron gave me.

I take the plunge. Innocuous blue sweatpants. Long-sleeved gray T-shirt. White tank top. Orange low-tops. A short-sleeved shirt with I HEART CARPINTERIA written on it. A pair of shorts. He did well. Then I reach in and find the last two items: a simple sundress that I would have picked out myself. Muted plum, just the right size. When I imagine him looking through the racks, choosing this one instead of, say, yellow, it occurs to me that he has been looking at me.

92

Or paying some attention. To get my style at least partially right. Then I find the last thing in the bag. A six-pack of leopard-print underwear.

I emerge from the bathroom—hair long and wavy, my eyes free from their brown murk, my skin glowing—to find Aaron asleep on the bed. He must've been waiting for me out here. It's the only bed, I kick myself for realizing now. I sit next to him and watch him for a minute, wondering what he's dreaming about. Lame groupies who send him their thongs in the mail? College girls who follow his Tweets as though they actually think they know the real him? Then I pinch myself. I sound like the jealous girlfriend. But that's an act I don't have to keep up.

"Hey." I nudge Aaron awake, grabbing the top of his sturdy arm. He doesn't move. I poke him. Nothing. Then, playing against type, I let my hair fall over my face and lean into him, placing my palm on his chest. I whisper into his ear, "Hey, lover. Watching you sleep makes me want to—"

Aaron bolts upright. "What? Huh? What?"

I laugh. "Well, I'm just living up to my underwear. I thought you'd be impressed. Playing against type and all . . ."

Aaron leaps off the bed like I'm a ghost. "Hey—that was all they had. I swear. That, or zebra." He chills out for a second. "Leopard's better than zebra, right?"

I nod. "Yeah." I pluck at the gray T-shirt. "They fit really well. Thanks."

"No problem," he says and begins to busy himself with lighting the oil lamps. "You look, um, good. Nice, I mean. Different."

My eyes widen. "No contacts." Then I realize he looks different, too. And it's not just his hair or his clothing or that we're in a cabin with just each other. He looks nervous. And for the first time ever—including our auditions, when I was a sure bet and he was the unknown—I feel nervous, too. If we were Jenna and Jonah, we'd burst into a ballad. So I try it.

"What song would work right now?"

He knows exactly what I mean. " 'Finally See the Light'?" he asks when a wick takes and an oil lamp warms the room with its glow.

" 'A Country Cottage with the Sea Below'?"

Aaron hands me a toothbrush from the desk and sings into his. "A country cottage ain't so bad, leaving the city behind, seeing the sea below . . ."

I pick up where his lame crooning leaves off. "I see the lights, but I can't see the stars . . ."

"But no matter where you go, I won't be far . . ."

I break the song and go out the door to the cabin's steps, where we both sit down. "I used to think of the most inappropriate plots for Jenna and Jonah," I admit. "Just to make it fun on set. In my mind? Like to keep my positive attitude."

Aaron rests his arms on his knees. "Like what?"

"Like . . . Jenna gets preggers and has the baby, but it

94

can't sing so they can't keep it." Aaron cracks up. I haven't heard him laugh so hard in ages, and I join in. "Or Mom and Dad go to a neighborhood party and swap partners, and we walk in on them and sing 'How Come Our Parents Are Big Sluts.' Things like that."

"You are so much more than I gave you credit for," Aaron says and then bites his lip like he can't believe he said it.

I turn to look at him, our eyes meeting, our arms almost touching. I really, really wish we'd never shared all those fake kisses, so we could start over. What if we were just a girl and a guy on a camping trip? I swallow hard and look up. "Hey—there's Cassiopeia."

"She said, breaking the tension that coursed between them," Aaron says, narrating.

"End scene," I say in a dead-on impersonation of our first director, who, like so many before him, succumbed to the idea that everything he touched would turn to gold. He's now behind the scenes of a pet-training show that films in western Connecticut.

"Why is it so hard for you to stop being 'on'?" Aaron asks, a mix of true curiosity and disappointment—he can't believe I went for the joke instead of being in the moment. Sometimes, neither can I.

I go from being lured in by him to being confused and unsteady all over again. It's nearly impossible to sort out the real between us and the scripted, allowing myself to feel something for him and fighting the suspicion that it might be a mistake. "It's called humor, Aaron. You should try it sometime—it's even better than sex. Oh, wait, you wouldn't know," I say and grin at him, but this time he's the one who can't let his guard down enough to laugh at himself.

Aaron bristles, his mouth screwed up tight, his arms tense. "According to the tabloids, you're the one who would know."

It's a cheap shot, but not unexpected. We're so familiar we know how to press each other's buttons when we want to. "Oh, is that right? Doing some heavy reading are we? And this from the guy who claims to have read *War and Peace* twice."

"Can you even spell *War and Peace*? You know it's not p-i-e-c-e, don't you?"

I reach out and thwack his shoulder. "Ha ha. Is that the same spelling as in 'You can't get a piece—' "

And again, just for a second I wonder if we'll drop the drama and he'll grab me and kiss me and I'll wrap my arms around him and feel his soft hair on my cheek. But Aaron looks up at the sky and then back at me as though he wished on a star that I'd disappear and he's surprised to find his wish didn't come true.

"This is ridiculous." He sighs and shakes his head. "We might just be everything that's wrong with Hollywood."

His words sting more than usual just because I don't know if he means the laugh track–infused *J&J* show, our acting ability, or just plain us—Charlie and Aaron, the noncouple.

Maybe he can't share my image of us together. On set or when we're being followed, I deflect his insults. Here, away from all that, my armor has been cast off and the venom gets to me faster.

"And here I thought we had a chance of being . . . ," I stumble, "*real* . . ." I look at him for some reassurance that he might feel the connection I do, but when he looks away, I just return to my backup plan—pushing him away. "I mean, that you had a chance of being a real human being. A man, even." This shuts him up, if only temporarily.

What would *Entertainment Tonight* say about us right now? What would *Stars!* or *People* deem noteworthy of this candid shot? Nothing. I look at Aaron, he looks at me, and we sit there in the quiet, with a nonexistent caption underneath:

Two kids attempting to be normal.

And failing.

10

THE STORY OF YOU

AARON

When I wake up the next morning, Charlie's gone, and so is the Rug Suckers van. I don't know what to make of this. I stumble down to the beach barefoot, and enjoy the feel of the wet sand between my toes.

Suddenly Charlie's at my side with two lattes in take-out paper cups. She holds the colossal one in her left hand and passes me the small with her right. "I guess you can have the small one this time, since nobody's watching. Mine's full fat with whipped cream and a caramel drizzle."

We drink our lattes and watch the waves. In the distance, I see a dolphin.

"So," she says. "Are you going to go back to Columbus?"

"Do you do that just to bug me, or do you really think there's only one city in Ohio?"

"You'll never know. So, okay, Cincinnati. Are you going to go back and sit in a rocking chair on the front porch of Old

Man Johnson's General Store with your hound dog at your side, or what?"

"First of all, he's not old, and it's Mr. Ochocinco now."

"What the hell are you talking about?"

"Johnson. He plays for the Bengals. Number eighty-five. He legally changed his last name to Ochocinco."

"I can't care enough about that to respond. So? Back to Ohio?"

"I . . . probably not. There's not . . . I mean . . . I guess I'll go to college or something. I don't really know what I'd do back at home. My little sister's a competitive gymnast and Mom's pretty wrapped up in that. And Dad . . . we love each other, but we kind of don't get each other, you know?"

"No. Not really. I mean, my dad lives across town, and I can't remember the last time I saw him. At least you get to talk to yours, and you know he loves you."

Charlie takes a long sip of her latte. The sea breeze has picked up and it's blowing in our faces. Which might be why Charlie's eyes are watering.

"Your dad loves you, Charlie. He talks about you in every interview."

"And you and I are a couple in every interview. You know? Just because somebody says something to a reporter doesn't make it true."

"But it doesn't necessarily make it a lie." And now it's my turn to take an extra long time sipping my latte and looking at the waves.

99

"I guess," Charlie says. "I just . . . I don't usually have this much time to think. I don't really like it."

"Why not?"

"Because I'm thinking about big things," she says. "What I want in life, who I want to be, without the input of agents or publicists who just want me to make them money. And I'm realizing that I don't know. I don't want to be a punch line in five years, you know? But most of the time, if you're a child star, you pretty much wind up forgotten by age twenty-five."

"I guess I never thought about that. I was pretty much always planning to retire as soon as I had enough money. Whenever that is. And then I guess have a childhood or something. Like, I worked so hard for such a long time, and I thought I was pleasing Mom, and I was, but now it's like— She's on to Michelle's meets, and I just feel like I was a project that she's done with. Like some moms do scrapbooking, my mother's hobby is pushing her children to elite status."

"My mom's projects usually involve plastic surgery."

"Well, she is hot as hell," I say. I know it's coming and step sideways to avoid it, but Charlie manages to land a punch on my shoulder.

"You are so gross. I can't believe you would say that about my mom!" She's smiling, but she hasn't stopped hitting me.

"Hey, so I rented *Beach Party Killer 2*."

"Oh my God, is that the one where her boobs are

hanging out the whole time?" Charlie hides behind her hair, then hits me again.

I put up my hands to block the punch to my shoulder. She's hit the same spot about five times. "That pretty much describes all five of your mom's movies." Her face is red and I think it's time for me to run away, so I flee up the beach toward the house.

"You've watched them all!" She's fast for someone with such short legs.

"Well, I fast-forwarded to the good parts, if that— Agh!" She has managed to clip my leg, sending me sprawling into the sand. I manage to turn faceup just as she plants herself on top of me.

I outweigh her and my longer legs give me enough leverage to throw her off of me, but where's the fun in that?

"No paparazzi means I can finally punch you in your smug face," she says, raising a fist but still smiling.

"Hold that pose," I say, digging in my pockets for my phone. "I wanna get that up on the Facebook fan page as soon as—" The smile drains from her face.

"You have a phone," she says.

"Well, I'm really trying to use the camera funct—"

"You!" And her face is really red now, spittle flying from her mouth as she screams at me. "Have! A! Phone!"

Oops.

11

THE STREETS OF LONDON

CHARLIE

Our highest-rated episode of *Jenna & Jonah's How to Be a Rock Star* was the episode that almost didn't get made. End of Season 2, Jonah was in his usual state of self-congratulatory confusion—should he go to the prom with the girl of his dreams (me, of course, played subtly in a beautiful dress and with downplayed boobs) or should he receive the Golden Frog Award (the Family Network's answer to the Kids' Choice Awards) or should he, rising rock star that he is on-screen, keep his tour date in the Bahamas? Never fear, dear viewers, he does all three! Shocker! Jonah convinces a pilot of his plight, gets the pilot to charter a private plane from the concert to the awards show and then back to my yellow house. Keep in mind his house is under construction, so he has to sleep over—but not, NOT, in my room. He can sleep in my brother's room, who is, of course, conveniently at an all-star pitching thing "upstate," even though we don't really know where on a map that would fall. But here's the best part: I was—I mean Jenna was—kept out of all the mass confusion and private planes and concerts for that episode. I was laid up in bed with a broken ankle (an injury sustained in real life, skiing in Vail—ask me if Fielding cared), narrating the show as it went along. Highest viewership ever for a Family Network show. And more people downloaded the final scene than watched live.

Cue the rain on prom night, even though the show is set in a fairly rainless make-believe state. Cue Jonah hurrying to put on his tux and scrape together a corsage from the rhododendrons in the yard. Cue Jenna (uh, me) lying in bed, having narrated nine-tenths of the story. The spotlight-generated moonlight streams in my fake bedroom window. A lone silent tear works its way down my perfectly made-up cheek. I continue to narrate: "So if you're wondering if Jonah makes it to the prom, I can't tell you that. Because I'm not going. Will there be other proms? Maybe. But right now, in the prime of my life, I'm sitting this one out." Cue full-length shot of me in my white nightgown, hair a tumbled mass, fake brown eyes watery, as my cast somehow keeps me from being able to crutch my way to the dance.

But—wait—what's that? It's the stirring chords of a power ballad as Jonah bursts through the window to sneak me out of the house and carry me in his arms—to the prom! Worried about my dress? I manage to turn my bathrobe sash into a bow and rip the sleeves from my nightgown in the limo and twist my hair up with the rhododendrons, inspiring many teens to rip apart shrubbery and tear their nightclothes to disastrous effect. Jonah saves the day! Jenna goes to the prom! The song shoots to number one on iTunes before the episode is even over. And the YouTube clip? Still one of the highest ranked.

Aaron finds me beachside this morning, bringing a mug of tea as a peace offering. I examine it but don't accept it yet. "It's green tea—antioxidants . . . Come on, you know you want it . . ."

I take the steaming mug—the sting of last night having faded a little—and sip it while staring at the waves as they break near my feet. "I always wondered why I didn't just use crutches in the prom episode," I say.

There's only a second or two when Aaron doesn't answer; then he nods, taking a few steps closer on the sand so we're side by side but not looking at each other. "I know, it's like, they wanted you to be stuck up there in the princess tower and I'm riding in on a black stallion to rescue you."

I sip more tea, abandoning my flip-flops on the sand and letting my bare feet drag in the surf. The cool water feels good on my skin. I sing, "Lying all alone, nobody on the phone, no one came for me . . ."

"Until you did," he half sings and then grimaces. "Ugh. I loathe that song—even if you sound decent singing it."

I continue, singing louder now and with my real voice, which can more than carry a tune. "But doors will open, windows, too; all I'm asking is you be you. Save me, come for me, I'll rise to the occasion . . ."

Aaron looks amused and slightly sweet, his stubble and sleep-tousled hair working wonders for him, and his expression is one of tenderness, as though the song doesn't bring up only evil feelings. "You're the first, the last, the only one, the one who makes me come undone . . . ," he sings and then can't help but laugh and comment, "I mean, is it just me or is it lewd? We're 'pure' neighbors? A love song? Rise to the occasion? Come undone?"

"You might be on to something. Or you just might be a perv."

"Well, that's a definite."

I laugh, loving the banter between us. More than anyone, he's the one who brings out my playful side, even if it's defensive sometimes. "It's funny. I always loved music—I guess I still do, except I hardly listen to anything anymore." Aaron nods and I go on. "It's like singing bullshit kind of sucked the enjoyment out of me."

"I actually removed the sound system from my car." He pulls off his shirt, shivering once and giving me an eyeful of his toned chest. The arms that have wrapped around me so many times look unfamiliar now. It's amazing how the light of day can make everything feel better, as though his accusations last night weren't really said by him. A body double maybe. "What use is music if all it does is make those lyrics echo in my head?" He turns to look at me once before plowing into the surf, swimming through the waves until he's yards away, bobbing in the morning light.

Normally, I'm not a swimmer. That is, usually I'm being photographed and therefore am not interested in being caught with pool hair or with my bikini half off, so waves and tides are not my thing. But here, free from watchful eyes and lenses, there's no reason not to swim. So I shuck my gray T-shirt, keep my bra and dazzling leopard underwear on, carefully set the teacup in the sand, and tentatively wade in. Aaron watches all of this, staring at me as the water rises up my legs to my waist, and I don't flinch.

We meet in shoulder-deep water. He raises his eyebrows, looking like he's about to tell me a secret.

"What?" I ask. "Never seen a girl swim in her underwear before?"

He tips his head back in the water and shakes his head. "Never seen you do it." I can tell he means he thought I was the type who wouldn't want sand or seawater to muck up her makeup. Why would he think otherwise?

"I never had the chance," I say. And then I can't help but follow up with, "God, everything I say sounds cliché, doesn't it?"

"It's not your fault." Aaron flicks water at me. "In fact, just splashing you feels cliché. Like now's the part where we get in a water fight and laugh and some upbeat song plays and then we get closer, splashing, and then—"

I swallow hard, looking at him, knowing that the end of

his scenario would end with a kiss. Something we don't do now. "So maybe we should do everything anticliché."

Aaron floats on his back and I do the same, looking skyward. "How do we do that?"

"I don't know . . . For starters, we should have a sad song in the background. Not an upbeat one."

"Like what?" he paddles over to me so he can turn his face and see mine. We look at each other across the dipping and rising ocean. "'I Used to Love Her But I Had to Kill Her'? That's Guns N' Roses. Or maybe no song but a shark comes and eats us both. That'd be unexpected."

"You really want to fade to black right now?" I ask and stand up. I touch his leg and for a minute we're there, in the ocean sounds—birds, waves, wind—and I wonder if I should splash him or what. The "or what" being more nerve-racking. And I want so much to still be angry at him for last night, annoyed by his smugness and his lack of respect for the job I've had my whole life, for sabotaging everything. He has a hometown to go back to; Hollywood is my everything—there's nowhere else for me to go. But maybe that's behind us now and we can move forward and figure out—together—what to do next.

Of course, just as I'm thinking this, Aaron comes out with, "You know, the problem wasn't about your leg."

I scrunch my face in confusion and the bright rays. "Meaning?"

"Meaning it was the show that was the crutch." He

crosses his arms over his chest and raises his eyebrows. After a second he rakes his wet hands through his hair so it's spiky but picture-perfect in that sea 'n' surf way.

I give him my "you've got to be kidding" look, all hands on hips and smirky, except my body is hidden under the water so most of the gesture is lost on him. "*Jenna & Jonah* wasn't a crutch—it was a job."

"See? You're using the past tense already," he insists. I want to throw up. It can't be past tense. Aaron goes on. "You used that show—"

I slap the water and groan. "They used me! It used me."

"Maybe, but you did it right back. And not for the paycheck—because we all did that. You did it so you'd never *really* have to challenge yourself."

I shake my head, trying to remain calm. "I can act." The words sound small.

Aaron cups his hands together, forming some sort of water fountain that spits ocean spew out at me. I duck. "Really?" Disbelief shows up all over his face. "You want to know why they had you lying in bed that whole time?"

I can still smell the production-set odor, hear the hollow sound of memorized lines reverberating in the set. I smirk. "I couldn't move. It's called a broken ankle."

"No! It was because you couldn't—can't—cry. The producers, Jerry and Marsha—they were panicked they'd have to use that fake tear shit like at the playground scene back in season one."

108

I wrap my arms around myself, stunned that I could have thought it was all behind us. All his condescension. His certainty that he's right and I'm nothing but a hack.

"It's not my fault I can't cry," I insist. I never do. On or off the set. "But it doesn't mean I can't act."

Aaron cocks his head. "Um, actually, the definition of acting is being able to sustain believable emotions regardless of the true feeling of the—"

"Oh, shut up! There's nothing about crying in there, Mr. Webster. It's not as though you've won a Golden Globe, either—hello, Limited Range. Look at me! I can glare! I can pout!" I put on my best Jonah impression and it's enough to silence my costar. Former costar. I try not to imagine the rest of the world, how it's spinning, how people are being hired, fired, let go from contracts.

"I just want you to be the best you can be, that's all," he says as though that excuses the insults. Maybe he does only want the best for me, but he has a funny way of showing it.

A few minutes slide by and we swim, not really with each other but nearby. Floating in the cold water, I watch a gull diving for its breakfast. So what if I can't cry? Tears are not the only measure of good acting. I had to cry on my first job, the diaper gig, and I managed that, right? But since then, I've faked it. And faking it is the definition of good acting.

Aaron wades over to me, waist deep in the water, striding as though he's got groceries on both hips. He's not looking as smug as before, so I relax but squint so he knows I'm still suspicious. But he bypasses any further critiques and his voice softens.

"So what song? If we were going against the cliché . . . Tell me." He bites his lip, submerges his entire body, and then stands up, close to me. Rivulets of water come down his cheeks to his jawline, and the air chills me, so I sink underwater to keep out of the air and make sure my nipples don't show too much.

" 'The Streets of London,' " I say. "It's really old. Some guy, Ralph McTell, wrote it. My dad used to sing it to me when I was little."

He furrows his brow and nods, really interested. "Oh, yeah? Did he play an instrument or just sing?"

"He just sang . . . but every night." I give a small laugh, feeling a bit exposed for telling the truth or anything about my family. "I couldn't get to sleep without it for a while."

"So sing it now," he says softly. "Give me the anticliché version."

I explain it first. "It's this guy and he's walking the streets of London and seeing day-old newspapers selling stuff that doesn't matter anymore . . ."

"You always do that," he says. "*Talk* about the thing instead of just *doing* the thing. Like when you wanted to take that trip to Europe? You brought those guides in and bored me to tears at the dumb bagel place talking about Belgium and Milan instead of just going."

"Well, I do kind of do that—probably because my mother

used to sell everything to me, to try to make me give in to her. She's a better actress than manager, and that's really saying something." I sigh. "But the trip's a bad example. I mean, I could hardly just walk out on my contract and our 'romantic getaway' to Tahiti."

Aaron nods. "So how does the rest of it go?"

I pause, feeling shy about singing. Then I realize why. We sing scripted pop songs. Not ones that mean anything personal, not ones that inspire genuine emotion. But I force myself to sing. "How can you tell me you're lonely, say for you that the sun don't shine?" Then I stop singing. It was always too expensive to buy the rights to use real songs on our show, which is one of the benefits of having original songs. "Then he says he wants to lead her through the London streets and show her around. Somehow this will make her change her view, you know, make everything different . . ." I immediately try to apologize, for what, I'm not quite sure. "Anyway, you'll probably think it's cheesy."

"You don't know what I think. We're off the page, remember?" He slicks his hair back and finds my hand under the water. "It's pretty. It sounds sad and sort of . . . I don't know . . . gentle." He looks down at the water and then right at me, his eyes locked onto mine.

"Aaron . . . ," I start, but I can't get words out.

His whole voice is different, cold. "See?" He breaks the gaze and drops my hand.

"See what?" I ask.

"That was me, just now, acting. Acting like I care." He raises his eyebrows and grins. "Pretty good, huh?"

I want to tell him he's an asshole. I want to slap him. The industry is so competitive and cruel, it really works its way into your bloodstream. It might be impossible to be normal after nearly drowning in it, and maybe that's why Aaron keeps reverting to his jerky persona. But instead of giving in to the dramarama impulses, I nod. "So . . . you think I need to improve, right?"

He nods slowly, deliberately, and waits for me to react with my usual fit. But instead, I give him a long, lingering look, my gaze taking in his wet chest, his shoulders. I step closer to him. Aaron narrows the gap between us, getting closer to me. Close enough that it would take very little to make us touch. But we don't. We can't. Or I can't, because if there's anything that the back-and-forth of reality and acting, that nice Aaron/mean Aaron has reinforced, it's that I should protect myself. Cue the splash fight.

I take his hand, sliding my fingers through his, making our hands entwine again in the warm underwater world. "So, Aaron, what's next?" I wait for him to drop my hand, to break the mood with a caustic remark, but he doesn't. With his eyes glued to mine, he pulls me toward him.

"Are you going to sing a power ballad?" I can't help but ask.

"And whisk you away to prom?" He grins.

"A girl can dream."

"Keep dreaming," he says, and to combat any of his

hesitancy, I loop my arms around his waist. He tightens his grip on mine, pulling my body into his. I stand on his feet, then wrap my legs around his waist so he's supporting me. He leans in, and I know his lips will be salty. His mouth will be warm and familiar but different, too, and I smile. He smiles back, a real soft smile, and leans forward. We're in the ocean, about to kiss for real, with only the sound of water and gulls around us. Closer. Our eyes meet. Our lips are about to touch and then I hear it. The sickening sound—roll film!— and a herd of paparazzi with telescopic lenses, reporters with their camera crews, the E! news anchor running on the beach in her high heels.

But before we can react to that, Aaron stares at me, still in the moment. "What do we do?" he asks as though we're really a team.

I break away from him and grin his own grin right back at him. "See? You know what that was? That was me. Acting like I was attracted to you. Pretty good, huh?"

I leave him there because it's easier to be alone, to do what I've always done and back away from getting hurt, to leave before I can be left, just in case everything Aaron does is an act. Deep inside I want to be with him. I love laughing and talking with him, love making pasta sauce and singing with him, but it's too much exposure for my heart. You just never know when you're going to get slammed with rejection. It's simpler not to get close, not to touch his hair, not to link hands and join forces. Easier just to wave good-bye.

12

SHE'S GONE

AARON

Cameras, reporters, and all, I really want to go running after Charlie and say I'm sorry, I don't know what makes me such a jerk, I shouldn't be so mean to you. But that would be embarrassing, both for the emotional display and because I'm still sporting visual evidence that suggests, given the proximity of an underwear-clad Charlie, that I'm heterosexual. So I decide to just hang out in the surf for a while until things subside.

But Charlie—I have to hand it to her—strides from the surf in her bra and leopard-skin panties and stands there for an interview with the paparazzi. Every mom in America is going to see those shots as they wait in line in the supermarket next week: Charlie dripping wet, wearing sexy underwear.

If she wants, she can probably turn this paparazzi moment into a *Vanity Fair* or *Maxim* shoot when she's eighteen.

Good luck to her. The relative cold of the water has taken care of everything that came up during our little faux-mantic clinch in the water, so I float on my back with eyes closed. The sea holds me up and moves me around. I hear Charlie's voice, I hear the shutters on the cameras clicking, but it's all background noise. I wonder if it's too late to put in some college applications.

Suddenly, Charlie's voice breaks through the noise. "Field! Field, honey! We're canceled!"

I raise one hand in the air, and while it's tempting to raise a middle finger, I give a thumbs-up instead. I hear the paparazzi laugh, and then they start tossing questions my way.

Why don't I get up and moon them? Why don't I just paddle out to sea and float to Tahiti? Why do I find myself walking out of the surf to join Charlie on the beach? No wonder Charlie doesn't get me; I don't really get myself.

"Fielding," a male voice says, "why'd you give the thumbs-up to being canceled? What do you have to say to your fans?"

Once again I ponder telling the fans the truth. "I have to say thank you. You've supported us for four years, and we would never have had the career we've had without your support. I'm sorry for disappointing you. But listen, folks, here's the deal. I'm . . . I can't speak for Charlie, but we've spent basically our entire high school years on this show, and I'm just kind of ready to move on. How many of you would have liked to do a fifth year of high school?"

"Not too many of us got paid for it," a male voice says.

"Hey, fair enough. But still. I mean, don't get me wrong, I understand how completely lucky I am. My folks still live in their house in Cincinnati, and they've worked hard for their whole lives and had very little to show for it. Certainly a lot less than what I have. And that's stupid and unfair and I'm ridiculously lucky, and all the same I don't want to do it forever. I'm ready for a new challenge. When we met Nicki, who toured the studio on what turned out to be our last day, she understood that we're real people and we can't be the same forever. Our fans are growing up, and we should, too."

I meant this whole speech as a peace offering to Charlie. Here you go, now go ahead and do your *Maxim* spread and grow up, and I can stop being Fielding. Finally.

"Are you excited about Shakespeare?" the *EW* lady asks me. I look to Charlie for guidance, but she's ignoring me, deep in conversation with *In Touch*, or maybe *Life & Style*.

"Uh. Well, I'm an actor. So, yeah, you know, I'm excited about Shakespeare in general."

"And how do you feel about being cast as Beatrice and Benedick? Is this the last chance to save your careers?"

I search the face of my inquisitor, trying to figure out what the hell she's talking about. Charlie's still not looking at me. "Well, I mean, we're a little young for Beatrice and Benedick, don't you think? I mean, probably Claudio and Hero would be a better fit, age-wise, but Beatrice and Benedick are really way more interesting parts."

EW lady is standing there with her mouth literally hanging open.

"I . . . ," she stammers. "I don't know . . . I mean, I'm not familiar—"

"Of course, actors are supposed to want to do the tragedies, right? But I have to say, I don't have any great yen to play Hamlet or anything. I'd rather play Puck, or Bottom, or Orsino, maybe even Prospero when I get older. I mean, why would you want to be Lear when you could—"

"Okay, we've got what we need," the *EW* lady says.

She walks away and the rest of the pack follows. Nobody asks me about being gay.

I'm alone on the beach with Charlie again. At least I am until she stalks up to the house. I guess I should be happy that she doesn't hang around to mock me for saying, "I don't have a yen." I walk slowly, hoping to be able to share information whenever she cools off, but by the time I'm back in the house and changed into dry clothes, she's driven off in the Rug Suckers van.

I take my phone off the charger and turn it on. It beeps for a solid minute as it registers all the texts and voice mails and missed calls from Jo.

I delete all of Jo's texts unread, which leaves only this one from James: *Shakespeare. Cool move. Snuggles dumped me.*

Sorry, I text back. *How are you doing?*

Awesome. He responds right away. *Being offered every*

gay role on the planet. And lots of dates, too. Often with pho-
tos attached. Want me to forward some?

I text back. *I'll pass. Good luck.*

I call Mom's cell, but she doesn't pick up, so I call the home phone.

"Aaron!" Dad yells joyfully into the phone. "Where you been hiding out? Never mind, don't answer that. Carpinteria. I just saw the photos on TMZ."

"Um, I'm sorry, I was calling the Littleton household? Is my dad around?"

"Charlie in that leopard-skin print—let's just say there are a ton of straight boys who probably would have killed to disappear with her for a few days. Kind of a missed opportunity there."

"Dad, I—"

"I'm busting your balls, kid. I joined PFLAG, you know."

"I didn't know that," I choke out as tears come to my eyes. My dad joining Parents, Families and Friends of Lesbians and Gays is so completely out of character that it says more about how he feels about me than just about anything else he could have said. It makes it kind of impossible to insist that he's joined this particular support group under false pretenses. "Thanks, Dad. That means a lot to me."

"Well, I just want you to know that we love you and we're very proud of you, and nothing can change that."

"I . . . I love you too, Dad."

"Listen, kid," Dad says, his voice shifting from tender

into the mode I'm a little more used to, "just stay away from gambling. Gambling will kill you. Also, you probably know this already, but guys are jerks. They'll cut your heart out and stomp on it just because they can."

Dad's been telling me to stay away from gambling pretty much since my first paycheck. This is probably because his brother lost everything he owned on a three-day bender at one of the casinos in Indiana. I've never bought so much as a lottery ticket. He's warned me before about girls liking me for my money, but this is the first time he's warned me about men being jerks. I guess he never thought he had to before.

"Dad, I don't think I have to worry about guys breaking my heart."

"No, of course not. Big celebrity. But be gentle with the boys. Just because they're guys doesn't mean they don't have feelings."

"Got it, Dad."

We talk for about fifteen more minutes, and I get updated on all the extended family drama that rivals anything going on in Hollywood.

It's the best conversation I can remember having with my dad, but at the end of it I feel like I'm about ten years old. Like I've just been playing a grown-up. Which I guess I have. I walk out of my room and into the empty house. The house that seemed like a wonderful, peaceful oasis now just feels kind of lonely and run down.

Charlie's obviously taken off and abandoned me here. I told her she could, and then probably drove her away by being a jerk, because—uh, well, I'm still working on that one, but I still didn't really want her to leave. I snap open my phone and am eight digits into her number when I hear the crunch of car tires on the gravel outside.

I snap the phone closed and go running outside to greet Charlie in the Rug Suckers van, only to find it's actually Jo's Lexus. Charlie is nowhere to be seen.

"Phone. Ever hear of it? Ever answer one?" Jo says as she gets out of the car.

"Uh, Charlie sucked it into the Rug Sucker," I say, not exactly lying.

"Well. Here," she says and throws me a brand-new phone. "It's charged, it's got your number, and I want you to pick it up when I call you. We've got a lot of work to do. Let me tell you exactly what's happening."

Jo strides into the house like she owns the place, and I follow her.

13

WHAT YOU DON'T KNOW

CHARLIE

Here are three ways you know you're in trouble in "the industry" (as in film and TV—Aaron always hates when I call it that because he thinks it sounds affected, but what does he know?):

1) You've been out of the tabloids longer than you've been in them.
2) You're no longer asked to endorse overpriced products that Hollywood people don't actually wear but market to middle Americans, thus making them feel inadequate and ugly. We conspire to keep the magic fixes of lighting and retouching to ourselves.
3) Your agent leaves you a note scrawled on a piece of gas receipt.

I haven't had to deal with number one until now. Even though the paparazzi were all over us in Carpinteria, they only tail us now a week later to get the pathetic shots, ones that run with headlines like "Fall from Grace" or "Washed Up at Seventeen." Gone are the swarms of photographers that have lined the entry gate so many times in the past. Missing the paparazzi is a huge warning sign.

Number two on the list is also happening now—for only a few more hours will I be able to claim Super Fit! sports energy bars, the cardboard snack of choice, as my fave brand.

And I whip off my sunglasses just to get a better look at Martinka's all-caps note on the gas receipt.

CHARLIE—
WHAT A MESS.
YOU LEAVE TONIGHT—FLIGHT TO PDX.
PICK UP RENTAL CAR AND FIND YOUR WAY
ASHLAND. YOU'RE DUE ONSTAGE AT 7AM
TOMORROW.
THE CAT'S ON THE ROOF— MARTINKA

The cat is on the roof is actually from an old story my dad used to tell me. I would visit him on the set of whatever crummy movie he was filming and he'd sit there in his cop uniform or baker's whites and he'd tell stories. This guy asks his neighbor to watch his cat, and when he calls the next day to check on him, the neighbor says, "Well, the cat's dead. It fell off the roof and got smushed." And the guy's all sad, like, why didn't you tell me in a kinder way? The point being, you're supposed to lead up to the bad news, say things like, well, the cat's missing, and then, the next day, say, we're awfully worried about that cat, it doesn't look good. Then, finally, when the person's good and prepared, you say the cat is on the roof, meaning the end is near.

My mind's a whir after reading Martinka's note and I try to process it all as I unlock the door. The alarm sounds for a second as I type in my security code. Aaron is the only other person who knows it; I had to give him access so he could do all sorts of clever things, like surprise me with flowers and "wake up in my bed here" (even if I was already on set). I go upstairs and begin to frantically shove clothing and personal items into my luggage.

PDX? A quick search informs me that's the airport code for Portland. As in Oregon. As in, what the hell am I going to be doing there? Presumably this is what the photographer meant on the beach, but like so many humiliating experiences so far, I have to learn the details of my life from *DivaStar Weekly*, which they send me despite the fact that I've never asked for a subscription. Luckily, I find mine in a heap of mail on the floor under the mail slot. Having been away, I see my house with an outsider's eyes and it looks like no one lives here. Not just that I haven't been here in a while, based on the mail and stale air, but like no one has ever lived here. I cast my eyes on this week's *DivaStar Weekly* and read aloud in my best Jenna voice ("perky and upbeat, with nothing to hide"):

> *After the scandal that rocked the* Jenna & Jonah
> *set, scarred starlet Charlie Tracker and Fielding*
> *Withers—still denying any issues with his*
> *sexuality—will test their acting chops at the Oregon*
> *Shakespeare Festival.* Much Ado About Nothing *is*
> *the main stage production this summer; the festival*
> *is the oldest and most respected in the country—pretty*
> *high standards for two teen dramarama stars who*
> *might do better in a summer stock production of*
> *Grease.*

I don't know which is worse: that my acting credibility has suddenly plummeted (maybe it's always been down at the bottom, but people were too busy ass-kissing to say anything) or that I'm heading to the middle of nowhere to do God knows what on a stage. I panic, my stomach rolling, my fingers shaking. I haven't performed live on a stage since I did a reading when I was twelve in a version of *Our Town* set in space. It was very Hollywood and had cool special effects, but it tanked with East Coast people. And even then I nearly vomited from stage fright. So I've got that going for me. Actually, it's not even clear if I'm acting or sweeping the stage. Martinka's note is vague, though the tabloids certainly suggest I'll be in a play. *Much Ado About Nothing?* At least I know the lines. But how can I actually speak the words with feeling when I clearly need to learn to act? I've read that play a hundred times. I don't need cue cards. The lines aren't the problem. Presumably no singing. But the challenge of acting outside of the *J&J* set looms ahead.

Jenna would try to look on the bright side. A change of scene! No annoying fans and photographers! No charade of fauxmance! No personal training, tan spraying, toning, macrobiotic eating, agent meetings! But I'm quickly overcome with reality: No real job! No money! Dwindling fame! Not to mention spending more time away from my beloved California-king-sized, hand-plucked-down-duvet-covered bed. And the small task of attempting to embody the role of a lifetime is something I never thought I'd have to face before I reached twenty-one. And there's no place to hide onstage. A live audience instead of a laugh track. Just thinking about Aaron's smirk makes my face flush with anger. I try to replace the memory of linking hands with him underwater with dunking him.

I zip my bag shut, take one look at my house, and realize it might be my last. If I'm let go from my contracts, there's no way can I afford the payments. I call a taxi to take me to the airport. As I lock the door and enter the security code, two things occur to me:

1) I don't have anyone to call to drive me to my
   flight unless I pay them. Normally, people have

friends or family do this, right? People who
send them off with hugs, magazines, flowers, or
at least a "good luck." But usually my agent drives
me. Or the studio sends a limo. I feel a pit
growing inside when I realize I have no one to ask.

2) Once, when we were between scenes of *Jenna &
Jonah*, Fielding and I sat in our chairs reading. I
was halfway through *The Buccaneers*, thinking
about which girl I'd want to play in the movie
version, and he had a book the size of a large
pizza on his lap. He turned the pages carefully,
lingering and *hmm*ing in the most annoying
way. I tried to see what book it was, and when
he realized I was trying to read over his
shoulder or see the spine for the title, he
crouched over it to hide the words from my
view. When they finally called his name for
his next scene, he slammed the book shut and
looked right at me. "Shakespeare. Complete
works. You wouldn't be interested." As if the
Edith Wharton I was reading was drivel in
comparison. Aaron left the Shakespeare there
on his chair, tempting me, daring me to try it.
And now I'd have to.

According to the navigation system on my rental car, Ashland, Oregon, is located 350 miles north of San Francisco

and 285 miles south of Portland, which is to say nowhere I want to be. I follow the directions into the Rogue River Valley, winding my way along the ocean and then farther inland through natural tunnels made of the tallest trees and their canopies of lush summer leaves. At a stoplight, I look at one of the tourism pamphlets I grabbed at the airport. At the foot of the Siskiyou and Cascade mountain ranges, Ashland has a population of twenty thousand. Twenty thousand? That's, like, an average line of people waiting for tickets to one of the *Jenna & Jonah* events. Wide-trunked trees topped with deep green line the big streets, the summer greens soft, each branch dark against the fading light in the sky. Another traffic light. How many could a town this size possibly need? I stop at the red and read for a second.

Ashland and the whole southern Oregon region offer every visitor a wealth of exploration and discoveries. From historic Jacksonville to the wonders of Crater Lake to local museums and wineries, there are cultural and scenic treasures awaiting you. We know your vacation is about more than the plays onstage—browse our attractions and accommodations listings and create your ideal Rogue Valley getaway.

Rogue Valley? Sounds like a perfect place for Aaron, though this is hardly my ideal getaway. I turn left toward Pine Hill Drive, which, according to the packet of information

Martinka had waiting for me at the airport, is where I will be living. When we were filming in Japan, we had an amazing house complete with meditation pools and koi ponds. And when we did that ChristmaKwanzikah special with the Inner-City Choir and the Disabled Kids Troupe, I had the entire top floor of the Mandarin in New York City. And even though I'm not into hotels—they're so impersonal, really—I'd gladly stay at an inn instead of 16 Pine Hill Drive, which is not so much the woodsy castle I had imagined. Rather, the structure is pretty much only that: a roof and walls to provide shelter from the elements. I stand there, studying the tiny Lincoln Log cabin in front of me and wondering what time I could catch the next flight back to LA.

"Cast or crew?" asks a guy in full-on Shakespearean garb. His hat has not one but two feathers on it, his tights—never a good look on a guy—are white even in the dark, and his accent is more Des Moines than London. "M'lady," he finishes.

"Cast," I say. And then I add, "I think."

He laughs. "You must be jet-lagged."

I nod, even though there's no time difference. Between the flight, the drive through the woods, and the loss of my familiar set and routine, I realize I have no idea what to do or how to be. And it's worse without Aaron.

"I have to run this codpiece back to costuming," the guy says, "but don't miss the midnight club."

A club? Maybe the place isn't as dead as it seems. "Is there a list?"

He looks confused, as though I'm speaking another language. "It's just desserts—leftovers—in the lodge." He gestures to a large, squat building on the other side of the clearing near the cabin. Lace flounces from his sleeve, making the action appear comic. "Sundays and Wednesdays," he adds. "Get settled and come on down later. We'll all be there."

"We," he says, as though I'm part of the *we*. I smile at him, grab my bags from the car, and wait until he's gone to walk up the steps. To the left, behind the cabin, is another just like it. And to the right, another one. It's like summer camp. Or the summer camp I've seen in movies. Maybe we'll sing around the campfire. Maybe hijinks will ensue—short-sheeting beds, shaving cream instead of whipped cream. I can almost hear the laugh track now.

In my cabin, I find a single bed, a dresser, and a functional though tiny bathroom with a shower built back when the festival started and mold that has probably lived through every show since. I walk over to the bed, hearing my flip-flops slap against the bare wood floors, and sit on the narrow, sagging mattress. The mugginess gets to me, finally, and I go to the window and fling it open. Outside, the moon rises behind the trees. I can't decide if the extra light makes the cabins and lodge look more like a fun summer camp or one of those camps where a killer lurks in the bushes, waiting to grab the campers.

My reverie is broken only by laughter. Guffawing, laced with a snort that can only mean one thing: Fielding Withers has arrived. Aaron. I leave my bag unpacked and rush from my stuffy room outside to welcome him. Even if he's not a friendly face, at least he's a familiar one, and costume-free. The screen door squeaks and I'm already planning out my opening line: How'd we get ourselves into this? Can you believe the town—it's like a film set of a small town, right? Did anyone follow you here? Miss me much? I don't dare say things that suggest I don't know if I can handle *Much Ado About Nothing*, or that I wish I were sure of what the future holds—no way could I possibly reveal any of that to Aaron.

His laughter continues right up until he sees me, at which point it becomes louder, tighter, at the top of his throat—his fake laugh. Only, it's not just for my benefit. It's for the person standing next to him. Of course it's a female, in a form-fitting dress that pushes her breasts up. I appear right as she's saying, "But the corsets—you wouldn't believe how tight they are."

I'm hit with an image of Aaron undoing a corset, tugging at the laces and finding her flesh underneath, and I swallow hard. Maybe I just wish I were the one wearing a corset. And maybe I hate that I feel that way. But I can't help it when I see him standing in that familiar way, one hand in his pocket, the other brushing his hair back.

"Looks like you found your way here no problem," I say, interrupting their interlude. The costumed girl doesn't know that what I mean is, same old, same old.

"I've never had a problem with navigation." Aaron grins,

his eyebrows raised. He leans in closer to—Juliet? Ophelia? "Juliet here helped." He nudges her and she giggles, heading off toward the lodge.

I shake my head. "We're due onstage at seven tomorrow," I tell him even though he probably already knows it.

Memories of four seasons on the small screen, endless line reads, separate-bed sleepovers, forced lunches, and lip-locks flash through my mind as we stand surrounded by trees, natural moonlight, and the distant sounds of laughter from the lodge. I watch him sling a worn blue duffel over his shoulder and pause as though he's unsure where to go next.

I thumb toward the cabin. "Welcome home," I say, trying for a mix of friendly and ironic.

Aaron looks confused. "Home? You mean, we're sharing a cabin?"

I can't tell whether this is an exciting prospect or a revolting one, so I try to sound neutral, but I fumble over my words. "No, I mean, I have my own cabin. Of course. It's not like we're neighbors anymore, right?"

"No—the show's over." Now he looks more confused. "But . . . aren't we still neighbors?"

"Sure," I say and try to explain. "But, I mean, it's not like we're sharing a bedroom—"

He blushes—at least I think he does, but it's hard to tell in the moonlight. "Wait—am I or am I not bunking with you?" He elbows to the cabin to the right. "That's me . . . us?" It's awkward and weird after our closeness in Carpinteria. I can feel the attraction and maybe he can, too, but neither of us will acknowledge it. At least I never would, because he'd probably choose that moment to lecture me about the finer points of acting or suddenly remember Episode 24 in Season 3 when I had a stomach bug and he held my hair back as I barfed in the tour bus.

"So . . . ," we both say at the same time, trying not to feel weird.

"So I'll see you in the morning," he says. I feel disappointed but hope it doesn't show. He studies my face. "Unless you meant—"

"No!" I say too loud and too fast, and he looks hurt now. "I mean, good night."

"And call's at six forty-five tomorrow. Everything's always fifteen minutes early."

We stand there looking at each other. Of course he isn't sharing a cabin with me. Of course call is earlier than I'd thought. But about one thing Aaron was wrong. The show isn't over. It's just beginning.

14

I'M AN OUTSIDER

AARON

I still don't get me.

First there was the fact that I let Jo bully me into doing this at all. "It's the perfect balance," she said. "You'll be working, really showing your chops, but at the same time you'll be off the radar."

"But," I said, "I just want to go to college. I'm not sure I want to do this anymore."

"Then this will be the perfect opportunity for you to get a feel for a very different side of the business. It's not all the Family Network, you know? We can totally reposition you. And if you decide this is the last thing you want to do, well, you'll be a fantastic Benedick, and the last notices you get will be along the lines of 'Wow! He's not just Jonah!'"

"Also," Jo continued, "you and Charlie—you're kind of a package deal here. If you pull out, she's done, and then you've made the decision for both of you."

That was the argument that actually convinced me. I don't want to be responsible for killing Charlie's career. Any more than I already am, of course.

Which is how I found myself on a plane, in a rental car, and then in a great little cabin with a little fireplace in the mountains.

This should have been something I really liked, but I found out that Oregon, or at least this corner of it, is a very cold place.

I wandered into the lodge, just looking for a snack, and found a bunch of people standing around. The place fell silent as soon as I walked in.

I scanned the room, looking for friendly faces. I recognized one guy who'd played our bumbling science teacher in two episodes of Season 3. "Hey," I said, waving.

"Look who thinks he can act," he replied and left the room.

"So, I guess we won't be reminiscing about our good times on the *Jenna & Jonah* set, then," I said. A few people smiled, but not many.

I walked over to the table with the food on it and got a wide, silent berth. "So, what's good?" I asked a crowd of younger actors nearby as I pointed at the food.

"When celebrities don't bump people with talent from parts they've auditioned for and earned," a young guy said.

Great. Jo had neglected to mention this, but of course these roles weren't vacant. Somehow Jo and Martinka cooked this up and got other actors booted out of the parts—Charlie and I are probably actually paying the salaries of the people we replaced. I knew people here would resent us for making a living as TV actors, but now they resent us for getting other "real" actors fired, too.

"Well, yeah, but since that's not on offer, I guess I'll just have a sandwich. Thanks for your hospitality, folks! I'll just be on my way."

I grabbed a hummus and veggie wrap and went back to my cabin, where I spent the evening rereading *Much Ado About Nothing*.

Until I heard a timid knock on my door at ten o'clock. I opened the door and found myself face-to-face with a gorgeous girl with long, auburn hair. She was dressed in sweats and not wearing makeup, but she didn't need makeup or a sexy outfit—especially since she was at my cabin in the woods alone at night.

"Hi," she said. "I'm, um, Steph. I'm playing Juliet? Can I . . . can I come in?"

"Yeah," I croaked out. All the saliva had drained out of my mouth, and though my heart was pounding, I felt kind of light-headed. This was probably because all the blood in my body appeared to be rushing somewhere other than my brain.

"I'd offer you something to eat or drink, but apparently every morsel I consume is going to cost me a fair amount of abuse, so . . ."

"That's okay," Steph said. "I'm not here for a snack."

She went and sat on my couch and patted the cushion next to her. I sat down. "I just wanted to . . . I guess I have a favor to ask you."

"Oh, I don't think I'd be doing *you* a favor," I said. "Believe me, it's been a really long time. I mean, not that I don't know what I'm doing or anything— I mean, I can certainly— I mean, wow. Sorry. Locked in this Charlie thing for so long, it's been difficult to—"

"Be who you really are?"

"Yeah. Exactly."

"Well, I'm here to help you with that."

"That," I said, "is awesome."

"Because," Steph said, "I need your gaydar."

"My—"

"You know. I'm playing Juliet, and Craig, who's playing Romeo, is totally hot, and I just really don't—I mean, this is stupid, right, but I don't want to make an ass of myself hitting on a gay guy. So I was hoping since you're here, you could . . ."

Steph will not be mine. Oh, well. She might at least be an ally in a pretty hostile situation if I play along. And though I'm not gay, I have worked in show business and palled around with closet cases for the last several years, so I do actually have halfway decent gaydar.

"Well, Steph, I might actually have to talk to him to figure that out, and if tonight was any indication, I'm gonna

136

have a pretty difficult time getting anybody to talk to me here."

"Don't worry about that. By tomorrow afternoon, probably at least half the people who snubbed you tonight will be handing you spec scripts and asking for your agent's contact info."

"Uh, okay, then. I'll see what I can do."

"Sweet!" Steph chirped. She kissed me on the cheek, bounced off the couch, and disappeared into the Oregon night, leaving me, as on so many nights before, with just my right hand for company.

The next day, despite Steph's prediction, turned out to be another day of me feeling, as my dad would say, "about as welcome as a turd in a punch bowl." I couldn't wait for Charlie to get here, to have someone to talk to who knows me, someone who doesn't hate me just for being me. Well, actually, I suppose Charlie does kind of hate me just for being me, but I guess that's it—everybody here hates me for being who they think I am, and only Charlie knows I'm loathsome for entirely different reasons.

So if I'm so comfortable with Charlie, why did I turn into a stammering bonehead when she arrived? What the hell was I thinking? I knew she had her own cabin, I just thought— Well, the blood-rushing-away-from-the-brain issue again, I guess.

Steph and I were joking about Craig—my gaydar having ruled him straight, we were joking about exactly what her approach was going to be, and I suggested just knocking on his cabin door at ten at night, especially wearing that, ha-ha, and then Charlie showed up.

And I probably made her incredibly uncomfortable. I'd kind of like to go knock on her door just to talk for a while, but now it would probably just be awkward.

I'm feeling pretty alone, so I call James on the off chance he actually answers his phone. He does.

"Oh my God," I say. "You picked up!"

"Yeah," James says. "Now that I don't have to pretend to be out clubbing every night, I've got plenty of time to stay home with the cats and watch musicals." He laughs. "Actually, I've gotten sucked into this Age of Magicke game."

"Uh. Cool?"

"It's totally not cool. But since I've moved from bad-boy leading man to hilarious best friend, I don't have to be cool anymore."

"Are you really playing hilarious best friends now?"

"Absolutely. Well, I'm actually going to be Sandra Bullock's hilarious gay *son* in her new comedy. But, yeah, it's pretty much cut from the hilarious-best-friend cloth."

"That's—that doesn't seem much like you to me."

"Of course it's not me! That's why they call it *acting*, genius! You're a little slow for such a freaking brainiac."

I laugh and pace the floor of my cabin. "Yeah, I guess I am. I'm just— Everybody hates us here for being famous, and they can't wait to see us fall on our faces, and I'm afraid we're gonna give them what they want."

"Listen. I am now pausing my game because this is important. Do you think the play you're in is better than *Jenna & Jonah*?"

"Only in the sense that Belgian chocolate is better than feces."

"Okay. So you made a connection with the audience when you were working with crappy writing. No offense."

"None taken."

"So why wouldn't you be able to do it with good writing?"

Because I'm good-looking and can sing and dance, but I'm afraid I'm not really much of an actor. I appreciate the sentiment, though.

I arrive at the rehearsal stage at six forty a.m. to find Charlie already there. She is doing her best "Chillaxin' with My Girls" (her hit single from Season 3) look, but I've worked with her for too long not to recognize the terror in her eyes. As much as she always goes on about being "born into the industry," I don't think Charlie has ever done live theater before. I know she's terrified about what happens when you don't get another take.

"Hey," I say. "I. You. That girl." Well, that was articulate.

She smiles. "It's fine," she says. "Sorry I showed up and blocked your—"

"Chances at helping her figure out if her costar is gay so she can hit on him?"

"Ha! Wait, she's not in *Othello*, is she?"

"No."

"Good, because that guy is old enough to be her dad."

"Anyway," I say, "I don't know if you've hung around enough to feel the full depth of everybody's hatred, but you and I are not exactly prom king and queen around here."

"I thought maybe you had just poisoned everyone against me before I got here."

"Did you really think I would—? Well, I guess I can see that. But they hated us both long before I got here."

"But," Charlie says, brushing hair away from her face and shaking her head, "I have three Teen Choice Awards!"

I laugh. "Yeah. Don't say that too loud or you'll get several colorful suggestions about where you might store those."

She smiles, and I'm relieved. She doesn't seem to still be mad at me, so our relationship is now a hell of a lot warmer than what either of us has with anyone else around here.

The other cast members have been trickling in and giving us the stink eye, and at the stroke of six forty-five, the director walks in.

She looks to be about sixty, she's got white hair down to her waist, and she's a little person. I mean, a Little Person. I mean, she's a little over three feet tall.

"Circle up, actors," she barks, and the entire cast of fifteen obediently stands in a circle on the stage.

"My name is Flannery Patrick, and this is my twentieth year with the festival. Last summer I directed the Public's production of *Midsummer* in Central Park. I could go on. The point is, I know what the hell I'm doing, and I'm good at it.

"You might also remember my performance as Villager Number Six in 1988's *Willow*. Or my remarkable work in the title role of *Goblin 2: Bride of the Goblin*. I reprised that role in *Goblin 3: Son of Goblin* and *Goblin 4: Revenge of the Troll*. Pretty much any time you see an old crone little person in the movies, that's me.

"Here's my point. Working actors do all kinds of things to put food on the table. I can afford to work for scale at the festival every year because I make very good money getting latex prosthetics stuck to my face and overacting in two or three horror movies a year. I ask that none of you judge me by my work in the *Goblin* series, and I won't judge any of you by the work you've done elsewhere. We all have the privilege to work together to bring one of Shakespeare's finest creations to life. No one here is above this work, and no one here is below it. Am I clear?"

We all nod, and I can't help smiling. At least the director is on our side. Sort of.

We go through the business of going around and introducing ourselves, and I learn a few things. One is that Kyanna, who's playing Hero, is smokin' hot and eighteen years old. Another is that Al, a rotund old white guy who's playing Leonato, Hero's father (the festival is proud of its race-blind casting, which is why an ugly old white guy can have a beautiful African-American daughter), used to be the fresh-faced rookie cop on some cop show in the seventies. A third is that Edgar, who's playing Dogberry—the drunken idiot constable—is the biggest snob in the place. He goes on for about ten minutes about how he's devoted his career to playing Shakespeare's clowns and fools, and looks at me and Charlie as he says, "Of course, I'm too busy with my craft to watch . . . *television*." He says the last word the way most people might say "diarrhea."

Everyone else introduces themselves, but I don't pay a lot of attention, because I'm trying to figure out how to play mine. Like, is it more obnoxious to give information everybody already knows or to assume everybody knows it? Eventually I settle on this: "My name is Aaron, I have a stupid stage name, but you may know me from my performance in the title role of the Bobbie Sterne Middle School production of *Oliver!*"

This gets a chuckle, which I guess is the best I could hope for.

Once the introductions are over, we spend the next two hours reading through the performance script start to finish. Charlie and I are playing Beatrice and Benedick, two loudmouths who mock everything, but especially each other, and get tricked into falling in love with each other.

Kyanna (sigh) and Calvin (who's got my gaydar beeping wildly and is therefore not really going to be competition for

Kyanna, I hope) play Hero and Claudio, the young lovers who are almost broken up by a stupid plot put together by Don John (played by Paul, who Charlie can't stop staring at). He hates everybody for no good reason except that he's the illegitimate brother of the prince, Don Pedro (played by Luis, who, as it turns out, played the troll in *Goblin 4: Revenge of the Troll*).

The plot, as the name of the play suggests, isn't really the point here. The point is the wordplay, and from my point of view the stuff with Hero and Claudio is a distraction from the real heart of the story, which is getting Beatrice and Benedick to see that their big mouths are blinding them to what their hearts want.

What this means is that Charlie and I are carrying the show. Not as much as we did on *J&J*, but the success of this play hinges on our ability to breathe some life into this complicated language. James has a point about this being good writing, but it's also a lot more challenging for the actors and, in the wrong hands, the audience. This isn't just "Aw, Jenna, not again!" It's fast-moving, witty dialogue by the best playwright ever to write in English, and reading it through, I'm incredibly intimidated.

I'm sitting there with a knot in my stomach as we break for lunch, and it's not made any better by Flannery, who says, "Charlie, Fielding, I need you for a minute."

Charlie and I exchange "uh-oh" looks as Flannery comes over to us. I decide now is not the best time to remind

Flannery that I'm going by Aaron now. I see Edgar lingering by the stage door, waiting to listen in as we get scolded for God knows what.

"I gave that speech at the beginning to get the rest of the cast off your backs, but your line readings were lazy. I know it's our first day, but you can't just breeze through Shakespeare like it's a Family Network script. You have to show the material some respect, and right now I'm not seeing that from you. I'd better see it this afternoon. Clear?"

"But—," Charlie starts to argue.

"We've got it, Flannery," I interrupt. "You'll see something different this afternoon, I promise."

"Damn right I will," Flannery says and walks away. I see Edgar snickering as he heads off to lunch.

Charlie looks at me, panicked, and whispers, "I thought I was showing the material respect! I can't show her anything different this afternoon! I don't have anything different!"

"Of course you do," I tell her. "You just have to dig deeper to find it."

I hope I've convinced her, but I'm not convinced. We might be in real trouble here.

15

THE BASIC EMOTIONS

CHARLIE

I pick at my Greek salad, wishing not only that the feta were organic, but that I had any idea how to act. All this time, I've thought my background, my commercial experience, my job meant that I could act. Now I realize that I can perform, but I can't act. After Flannery's pointed remarks about my lines this morning, I sit on one side of a wide patio under the shade of a huge tree and feel pathetic. I stare up at the tree for inspiration, thinking that if this were a scene in a film, I'd find enlightenment beneath the leaves. Instead, all I find is embarrassment—I don't even know what kind of tree it is. I stare up at the branches as though this will tell me.

"Buckthorns," the fat old man says. He carries himself like a cop, which is probably why he played one on TV before I was born. Studying his creased face, I also remember he hawked paper towels. I fight the urge to say, "Gets the wetter drier better," which was the slogan.

"Buckthorns?" I say back to him as he deposits himself into a chair. I don't know if that's his name or a line of dialogue, and I'm feeling dumber and dumber by the minute. I hunch down in my chair, resting my elbows on my knees as though shrinking will make this world I've stumbled into disappear. Looking at him, I feel a mixture of awe and pity; he's a veteran in the industry and yet now he's reduced to doing small-town Shakespeare when he used to win Emmys. Maybe it's better to be like my dad and always do crap. Both my parents seem content in their mediocrity; no one expects much from them. No one's waiting for them to fall.

"The trees. They're buckthorns. *Rhamnus* in Latin, but I don't suppose you speak Latin?" His gray blue eyes are gentle; his voice sounds as though he might have only recently kicked a pack-a-day habit.

"I don't, um, speak Latin . . ."

"But the question is—can you play someone who does?"

I twist my hair up off my neck and squish it into a messy knot to cool off. Off to the side, Fielding-Aaron sits with the few actors who will deign to speak to him, and inside in the air-conditioning Flannery and the heavy hitters eat lunch together, roaring with laughter that's audible through the French doors.

"Actors always outdo each other with their stories. I've been there too many times—I don't need to sit in there and hear the bullshit fly," the guy says, following my gaze. "I'm Al, by the way."

"I'm Charlie," I say, grateful he reminded me of his name. Normally, stars have assistants to remind them of names. Martinka wanted me to hire someone so I wouldn't have to pay attention to other people, but I never did. Then I add, because he could be Jenna's long-lost grandpa, "I don't know if I can do this."

Al nods, his white hair falls onto his forehead, and he tries in vain to make it stay put. "Listen. It takes three things to be a success." He breathes deeply and coughs before going on. He holds out a thick finger for each item he lists. "Luck." He eyes me. "Which you got . . . Hard work, which you're also familiar with—I remember those hours on set. Nothing easy about that."

I sigh and nod, relieved that at least someone here knows what working on a television show actually entails.

Al continues. "And the third part of success is . . ." He raises his eyebrows and smirks. "Talent."

Birds sound in the trees behind us. I don't look up, but I wonder what kind of birds live in buckthorn trees. I wonder if I have the third thing.

"Most people in this business got two out of three. They're terribly talented but have no luck so no one finds them. Or they're rubbish actors but very lucky. Or they work very hard but they're talentless."

"And what am I?" I ask like Al would have any clue. "I mean, I want to have all three."

Al nods as Flannery rings a bell. Somehow, the experienced

cast knows this means lunch is over. "Take this," Al says and hands me a thick book, its pages yellowed on the edges, the cover worn and ripped in the corner. "It's not the answer. No one thing is the answer. But it might help."

I hope it's not a Bible. I've had many people try to convert me. I look down at the title. *Acting from Within.* I smile. "Thanks, Al."

He stands up and pats my shoulder. "It was a gift from my first director to me, and so I give it to you."

If we ever get out of here, I think, I'm demanding he work on *Jenna & Jonah.* Then, with a smack of reality, I recall there's no production schedule. There's no anything. It's O-V-E-R. "See you onstage?" I ask.

"Of course, Beatrice." Al bows. "But not for a few hours. Your call's later."

He eyes the tree again. "Buckthorns, as their name suggests, have spikes . . . but the Oregon species don't." He gives me a meaningful look. "Just thought you should know."

I hold the book to my chest, feeling as though I have a secret, and shovel my salad in so I can go read in peace.

I take *Acting from Within* to my cabin. Inside, the dim light is welcome but the stifling heat is not. Maybe lack of creature comforts is good for the soul, I tell myself, and begin to read. *What are the basic emotions?* I sit there on my bed, wondering. Love? Hate? Anger? Fear? Sadness? *Prepare a gesture that goes along with each of the words.*

I stand up. Love? What's a gesture for that? A hug? No, that's more kindness. I sigh in frustration. "What about hate?" I ask aloud.

"What about it?" I hear Aaron's voice before I actually see him. He sticks his head in the door and grins.

"Nothing." I immediately slam my book closed, but not before Aaron sees it and grabs it, holding it above my head.

He reads it as he keeps it out of my reach. "Present your gesture to the rest of the group. Try to feel the emotion as it arises from the experience of the gesture . . ."

I give up trying to grab the book. "Never mind." I wasn't good at the exercise anyway, so I might as well give up. My stomach turns over thinking of being onstage, with Flannery yelling at me about my lack of respect for the character.

"No," Aaron insists. "Let's do this." He doesn't look happy about it, mostly resigned, his scowl hidden behind his flushed face. "Let's see . . . five basic emotions . . ." He pauses, thinking. "Horniness—" He laughs. "Does that count?"

"Not unless you're acting the part of the prick," I quip. I notice how my body snaps to attention when I say this, my posture erect.

He falters, but only for a moment. He leads me out into the living room and stands with his hands behind his back in front of the unlit fireplace. "There's hate, anger, fear, sadness, trepidation—"

"That's the same as fear—at least for this exercise."

Aaron sways as though he hears music I don't, his mouth

twisted to the side. His T-shirt shows sweat marks from his abs, and for a fleeting moment I think about the cool water near his place in Carpinteria. How his hands felt under the water.

"You're forgetting love," I tell him.

He looks like I've slapped him. Then he regains his control and looks pissed, his jaw clenched. "I didn't forget it. I misplaced it."

"Perhaps it's in your pants," I suggest. I could get used to these verbal sparring matches; they're so much better unscripted.

"How's this for a gesture of anger," he asks and shows me a finger.

"Not very creative, but then, what can we expect from a fading television star?" He swipes at the air. "That's a better gesture." I snag the book and read aloud. "Now we imitate it." I do and Aaron starts to grin, but then grabs it back and reads more.

"Repeat the gesture exercise above, this time using a different emotion, which you express in a gesture plus a nonverbal sound." His voice is loud in the small, airless cabin.

Sunlight speckles the room as we work our way through sadness—which I communicate with my head down, shoulders dropped—and fear, which is surprisingly difficult to do.

"Come on, you look like you're on the run from a B-movie psycho killer," Aaron complains as I hold my hands in front of my face.

"Well, psycho killers around a lake are scary," I say.

Aaron approaches me suddenly, his eyes wild, his mouth in a snarl.

"What about in a small cabin in the woods?" I gasp and hunch my upper body down. "See? That's fear!"

He repeats my gesture, adding a nonverbal unsteady groan, and I do as the book demands. "Repeat the gesture-plus-sound exercise or choose a different emotion, now adding a single word or short phrase to the gesture and sound," I read, then perform it, hunching down, gasping, and adding, "No, please!"

Aaron sits on the arm of the couch and does his nod that looks like a chicken—head out and back. "The 'please' was a smart choice," he says. I sit on the floor, looking up at him, my arms crossed over my knees. "It sort of made a character."

I nod, excited. "That's what I thought! Like, just with one word, you could tell she was scared but also that there was something more than just not wanting to die, right?"

Aaron agrees, tapping his flip-flops against the bottom of his feet while he thinks. He chews on his thumbnail, which he can do now that there aren't any close-ups of him playing guitar. "She's probably cultured, or polite . . ."

I tilt my head back and forth. "I think there's more than that. When I add the 'please,' it's because she has something else that she wants to live for, beyond the 'Please don't murder me with a hacksaw in the woods.'"

As we sit there in the heat, sweat beading on our lips,

pooling under my bra, the faintest nibble of a feeling starts in my chest. Aaron looks at his watch. "We should make a move. Flannery'll be even more heavy-handed with the criticism if we're late."

I start to stand up and he offers his hand, yanking me a bit harder than is necessary, and I go flying forward, landing squarely against his chest. There's a second or two of bodies pressing together before I steady myself, and Aaron covers any awkwardness by doing the fear gesture again. "Gasp! Help me—my career is attacking me!"

I fire back at him with, "Please, no! I'll never get laid again!"

Aaron twists his mouth in retaliation, but comes up with nothing as we head out the door.

It's only when we're halfway to the stage that I realize we never did come up with a gesture for *love*.

16

HALF A BOY AND HALF A MAN

AARON

Apparently Flannery did some intensive work with Edgar on the whole Dogberry thing right after lunch, and apparently it didn't go well. As we pass him coming off the stage, he's muttering something about "pint-sized tin-pot tyrant wouldn't understand this role if Will Kemp himself . . ." He's too angry to even sneer at us.

We begin by simply blocking out the scene. It's a relief, because if there's one thing that even the worst actor on any two-camera sitcom can do, it's hit a mark. Charlie and I have spent the last four years crossing to X's both visible and invisible on the floor, so this is a breeze. We've both got our scripts appropriately marked, which hopefully impresses the other cast members, who keep casting sly glances over our shoulders to see if we know what we're doing.

Once the rough blocking is done, we run through the scene, which serves as a basic introduction to most of the characters and also to the "merry war" between Beatrice and Benedick.

"Now remember, you two," Flannery says. "You both think you can't stand each other, but there's not a single other person on earth who gets you the way the other one does. Why does Benedick not even cast an eye on Hero? He's a better match for her than Claudio. It's because nobody else will be able to banter with him the way Beatrice does. And Beatrice shows no interest in Don Pedro or any other man because she knows they would all be baffled by her. And yet, for all that, you drive each other crazy. Got it?"

My face is hot after this speech, and Charlie's tan face has turned pink. "Got it," I say, and Charlie just nods.

And we nail the scene.

"Courtesy itself must convert to disdain, if you come in her presence." Charlie sneers at me.

And after she swears she'll never marry, I find "God keep your ladyship still in that mind! so some gentleman or other shall 'scape a predestinate scratched face" a pretty easy line to deliver.

We spend the scene squinting at each other in disdain, but this is the most fun I've had acting with Charlie, or acting at all, really, since—well, I guess, ever.

The scene ends, and our fellow cast members are all staring at us, mouths essentially agape.

"Yeah, surprise surprise," Flannery barks. "Professional

actors can actually act. Close your mouths, everybody, we're not done for the day yet."

I really wish Edgar were here for this, but I have to settle for the newfound respect on the face of pretty much everyone in the room. "Aaron, Charlie. You're still doing TV acting—you're relying on these facial expressions that people in the cheap seats won't see anyway and not getting your body involved enough. Remember—no close-ups in the theater, so you can't sell a line with an arched eyebrow."

Well, she certainly doesn't give us an opportunity to get cocky.

After another two hours of rehearsal, I'm exhausted and I still need to go study my lines. I understand why they don't have TVs in the cabins.

Charlie is heading toward me when Kyanna bounds up to me and says, "Hey, a bunch of us are going to hang out later—just chill, maybe—" She makes the universal "smoke some weed" hand-to-mouth signal. "You wanna come?"

"Uh, well, I— Yes, I do. Where and when?"

"Just show up at Steph's cabin anytime after nine."

"I'm totally in." Well, I'm in for hanging out with the hotties. The pot smoking, not so much. The morals clause of our Family Network contract was pretty explicit about drugs (it actually listed the substances we were not allowed to consume, in both their technical and street names, along with "any illegal intoxicants or controlled substances that may be developed or discovered in the future, throughout the universe"). I admit that when I first got to LA, I thought it was a pretty big rip-off that I didn't get to party like the rest of young Hollywood. And then I started seeing at close range what partying like that does to people. How they get really old really fast, and before they know it their mug shot is on the front page of The Smoking Gun and that's the last time anybody hears of them. The hell with that.

I guess I was a little surprised at Kyanna's hand signal, but then again, we are in Oregon. It would probably be more surprising if people weren't smoking.

I stare as Kyanna bounds off, and apparently I spend too long watching her butt, because Charlie punches me in the arm.

"Ow! What the hell!"

"You know, for a master thespian, you really suck at pretending you're not interested in someone. You can't just *devour* a girl with your eyes like that. They don't respond to that!"

"Surely it's different when it's someone young like me and not the geriatric types who typically hit on you."

"Geria— Listen. I'll have you know—"

"I know, some of your stalkers are as young as forty, and aren't *technically* geriatric, but—"

"The first guy was twenty-seven!" she spits out, her cheeks reddening just a bit. Her lips curl into a sneer as she says, "And it's not like— Geez, since you came out of the closet,

I've gotten more fan mail from hot guys probably than even you have!"

"I am not getting tons of mail from hot guys."

"Wow, so your gay fans aren't hot? I am totally calling Perez Hilton with that little nugget. That'll kill whatever tiny bit of popularity you have left." Charlie's eyes are alight and her hands are clenched into fists.

"No, I meant that the people who choose to reach out to me are typically—"

"Ugly gay men. I get it." She's smiling triumphantly.

"Girls!"

"Yeah, not in the last few weeks, they're not. Call Jo. Ask her. She's probably the only straight woman still interested in talking to you."

"Kyanna just invited me to"—I do the joint-smoking pantomime—"hang out!"

"She probably just wants you to help her figure out if Craig is gay. She's not interested. I can tell you exactly how this plays out. She gets all close and chummy with you, and probably kind of touchy-feely, too, because it's safe, and then you make a move and she goes, 'Whoa, sorry, I thought you were gay. I didn't think it was possible to lead you on!'"

Okay. Charlie pisses me off at least three times a day, but never more than when she's right. She's got me on the conversational ropes here, and I need to strike back.

"Well, maybe she just thinks I haven't met the right girl

yet and she can be the one to change me. After all, I've only been seen in public with *you*."

Gotcha. Charlie's cheeks go from pink to crimson. "I am . . . Dammit, I was number six on the Hot 25 Under 25 list! If anybody could turn you straight, it would be me!"

"And yet, sadly, it didn't work. I'm just going to have to look elsewhere." I'm smiling now, and so is Charlie. "Good luck with Al."

"Al's mentoring me, dickhead."

"Yeeeah. Mentoring. Is that what they call it in Oregon?"

"Rrrgh!" Charlie storms off in the direction of her cabin.

"You wanna run lines?" I call after her.

"Yes! Give me half an hour to shower and stop being sick of you!" she barks back.

I arrive at Charlie's cabin. She's wearing a little tank top, and there are beads of water from her wet hair glistening on her bare and perfectly tanned shoulders. I'm not immune to this—she's right; she was number six on the Hot 25 Under 25 for a reason.

"It didn't work," Charlie says as soon as I walk in.

"The shower? You certainly don't reek anymore."

She glares at me. "No, the half hour. I'm still sick of you."

How can she be sick of me? She's the annoying one! "Well, I was sick of you for four years, and we managed to work together anyway, so let's do this."

"This" is our section of Act 2, Scene 1. It's a masquerade

ball where Benedick dances with Beatrice, pretending he's somebody else. I don't really care for this scene, because Beatrice totally gets the best of Benedick—she talks about what an ass he is, and since he's pretending to be someone else who doesn't know Benedick, he can't even get her back. It's definitely the round that goes to Beatrice.

I slide my hands around Charlie's waist. It does occur to me to slide a hand down to her butt, eighth-grade-dance style, as a joke, but since she's still pissed at me anyway, I decide not to. We waltz around her cabin. "This was Signior Benedick that said so . . . ," Charlie says.

"What's he?"

"I am sure you know him well enough. Hey," Charlie says, breaking character, "does she know she's really dancing with Benedick even though he's disguised? I think she knows it's him."

I sigh, exasperated. "Of course she knows it's him! That's why she's able to dis him so effectively!"

"Okay, okay!" She pulls out of my embrace and storms to the other side of the cabin. "You know what your problem is?"

"Everybody thinks I'm gay?"

"No, you love the attention. That's not a problem for you. Your problem is— Well, you know what *my* problem is?"

"They don't have the correct brand of mineral water stocked in your fridge?"

"Rrrgh!"

That was a pretty cheap shot. If it weren't for me and my alleged gayness, she'd be comfortably in her dressing room at the studio with all the mineral water she could drink. She closes her eyes, takes a deep breath, and then says, through gritted teeth, "No. My problem is I don't really know how to act. I know how to memorize lines and blocking, but I don't know shit about how to really find a character and become that person for two hours."

That's a stunning act of verbal jujitsu. She's just taken my best ammunition away, turning her weakness into a strength.

"But I'm still better off than you," she continues. "You know why? Because I *know* I suck. And I'm working on it. But you're so high on yourself that you don't even see that you're still doing Jonah. Benedick is a war hero! He's seen some horrible stuff! He's not some wide-eyed teen with a smart mouth like Jonah! But you know what? I know why you can't find this character. You can't find this character because Benedick, for all his flaws, is a *man*. And you just don't have that in you."

I turn to leave. The hell with this. "Well, I guess it's true that I'm not as much of a man as you, but few people are," I say as I turn to leave.

"Wow, that was mature," she calls after me as I walk down the path away from her. "You're proving my point, little boy!"

I raise a middle finger without looking back.

. . .

I grab a portobello and goat cheese sandwich and head back to my cabin. I don't know what the hell to do. I'm too angry to be good company to the hotties getting together to smoke—people getting intoxicated are amusing when I'm in a good mood and infuriating when I'm in a bad mood. Great. So Charlie has, in the space of just a couple of minutes, a) sabotaged my performance by planting these seeds of self-doubt that might well undo me and b) sabotaged my chances with Kyanna by pissing me off so thoroughly that I'll be sure to snap at the next human being I encounter just to have an outlet for my anger.

At home I would take a night walk on the beach, but out here there are mosquitoes the size of my head, not to mention the kind of complete darkness at night that you never see in LA, as well as God knows what kind of animals and Blair Witches lurking in the woods.

I have nothing to distract me. So I have to do something I hate—ask myself if Charlie might actually be right.

17

BRILLIANT DISGUISE

CHARLIE

Nothing prepares me for the fall. Like those dreams in which I start out being able to fly, only to look and see that I'm on a set of some kind with cue cards I can't read and an audience that looks bored, and suddenly I'm plummeting.

Only this time it's real.

The morning started fine. I slept decently after a line read with Aaron, even though it's exhausting having Benedick insult my looks, my personality, and my intelligence. Anyway, I am trying to hold my own.

But right now, I'm not living up to the task.

"Are you sure I'm not going to fall?" I ask the harness guy. He gives me a look that I try to memorize since it sums up the stupidity of my question. Of course I'm going to fall.

"Okay!" Flannery yells into a megaphone. "Beatrice on platform two, Benedick on three!" Yards and yards away, I see Aaron give his ready signal—sort of a glorified salute that informs the circus crew he's ready. Other cast members, our director, Al—everyone—waits for me. I look down. How many feet from the ground, exactly? My feet are bare, perched on a napkin-sized platform. I can ignore the heat even though sun and a bodysuit are not happy companions, but I just can't commit to the fall.

"I say again," Flannery echoes into the megaphone. "Are we ready?" Already Hero shakes her head; Claudio seems to be laughing, but it's difficult to tell from here.

"What's the point of this again?" I ask, forgetting I have a microphone clipped to my harness.

"The point," Flannery announces to everyone, "is that the director is telling you to do something."

"The point," Aaron pipes in, "is to let go."

But I don't want to let go. Isn't that my survival instinct? To hold on to life? Where is it written that I have to willingly bound into the air when, last I looked, I am not a bird?

I see some scurrying and Al speaks into the megaphone, his voice calm. "You aren't a bird, Beatrice. You know that." Al would know—he's told me tales of his rise from unknown sandwich maker to the stars to small film roles to the television role of a lifetime, the one that made him the cop we all thought we knew. He knows about dives, like when his show fizzled, how bad the response was when they tried to make it move from small screen to large. So I trust him.

I take a deep breath, happy that at least Al recognizes what I'm feeling, even if he went against his doctor's waiver and nearly flew across the air, jousting and jabbing and running his lines perfectly, making even his lumpy bodysuit seem regal.

"One emotion can cover up another," I say into the mic.

Flannery flaps her arms, frustrated.

"Just go, Charlie!" Aaron whines. If he were closer, I'd slap him. Now that's a gesture of frustration. Only, who am I frustrated at: him or me?

The cabins are way off to the right, the stages cloaked by tall trees and foliage. All that exists here are these tiny platforms, safety netting that looks worryingly flimsy, and us. Actors.

Al intones, "Yes. One emotion can cover another. Disguise it."

"Surface emotion versus hidden emotions," I think, remembering the reading I did last night. How it made me think about laughter covering fear, or haughtiness masking insecurity. How I used to demand silly things on the *Jenna & Jonah* set—water iced to a certain degree before I'd drink it, or certain skin creams even though they were just props— and how maybe that wasn't about what I thought. That maybe some of the power trips stars pull are just to get control over something. You can't demand people watch your show or control the opening weekend gross for your movie or what part you'll get next, but you can damn well insist that the crew not look you directly in the eye or that you wear new shoes every morning or that sugar is banned from the set.

I stare out at the emptiness that separates me from Aaron. From Fielding. From Benedick. Who, as far as I can tell, is no closer to becoming a man than he was before.

I yell, "Fear," and jump into the air, falling nearly twenty feet before I'm yanked up by my safety harness. Giddy with the rush of adrenaline and bravery, I keep going. Aaron says his line, calling me a parrot-teacher.

I continue the metaphor with, "A bird of my tongue is better than a beast of yours."

Aaron swings toward me, hair flying, his trapeze tucked under him. "I would my horse had the speed of your tongue."

Our insults bite, dig into each other as we careen toward each other, speeding into verbal danger and then away from it. My body feels free, and soon I'm able to gesture while flying, sweeping my arms at him like I'm trying to shoo him away, which is what Beatrice wants. Then, just as quickly, Aaron reaches out for me and I fall for it, allowing him to take my hand only to be reminded that he wants to "die a bachelor." It stings, especially because Beatrice has been down this road before—she and Benedick had been involved romantically but he left her. So she masks her hurt with wit.

"What say you, Beatrice?" Benedick asks, flying toward me, arms outstretched.

Suddenly, he's not Benedick; he's Aaron, and we're in the little cottage back in Carpinteria and he's sleeping. I remember the look he gave me when I woke him. In my legs I feel the weight of his hand on my thigh. How I thought it was real then. Then the cold shock of swimming with him and the camera crews and the first real kiss that never was.

I snap back, flinging myself away from him so Aaron's left dangling, alone in his bodysuit, between the two platforms, while I'm out of danger, safe on my little perch.

Act 2. Scene 1. Thunder drones overhead while inside Kyanna and I discuss our ideal guys. Of course this is not something I'd choose to do. I've never been one of those girls who takes quizzes about relationships—are you a traditional romantic or up for flirty fun? But while I was jumping around in the air, Flannery had Kyanna come up with a ridiculous list of questions meant to inspire our scene.

Kyanna drags her chair so it faces mine. Her ice cream sundae is beginning to melt, so she scoops the soupy stuff into her mouth while she talks. "Would you rather a guy a) bring you flowers for no reason or b) surprise you at work with plane tickets or c) leave you a love note on your pillow?"

I eye her ice cream and tap my foot. This is what it's come to? Telling a stranger my romantic fantasies? I stall. I want to act, just jump into my scenes, but Flannery insists we follow her roundabout routines—trapezes, quizzes, a group hike, all while thinking of our characters and working on lines.

"Come on," she says. "These kinds of things happen all the time with stage actors. You just do it. Some directors want to keep you away from each other, to build tension; some want you to share an apartment so you maybe end up really in love and then act it out onstage. You've heard of Sven Svenson?"

Normally, I'd nod and pretend I do, but I have nothing to lose, so I admit, "No. Never heard of him."

She raises her eyebrows, eats a cherry from the bowl, and tosses her braids behind her shoulders. "He's like the . . . Martin Scorsese of theater—respected, old guard, but always pushing it. Anyway, when I was fourteen, he had me do two weeks of boot camp. With guys. In Alabama."

"For a role?" I look at her, shocked. She nods. "Talk about devotion."

Kyanna grins, licking her lips. "It's what you do, right? Get absorbed by the role. Taken by the lines."

"You've been doing this a long time, too?"

"Since I was six. Started off in *Annie*—yep, I can sing. Played that little orphan Molly. Then went to school in New York and . . . one thing led to another, and now I'm between Broadway and West End shows, so here I am in Shakespeare land. Only, playing a supporting role because it's better for the long term, you know, the slow build?"

But I don't know the slow build, because my career was jump in, all or nothing. And I don't usually fawn, but I can't help it. "So you just do this all the time?" Kyanna nods. "All the lines, the . . . soul-baring . . . the intensity?"

"I could say the same to you—I mean, I know everyone downplays it, but it's got to be tough pretending to be the same character all the time." She sets the bowl of ice cream on the floor and picks up her script from her lap, paging through. "Don't you ever forget who you are in all that Jenna-Jonah world?"

I don't answer. If I'm truthful, I didn't forget who I was in Jenna so much as sort of blur the lines of who was who. She was me. I was her. We started off so low, with no expectations on a small channel with no viewers, and I did whatever I wanted with the character without much effort. Now I'm in exactly the opposite situation. I wonder if Aaron feels the same.

I pick up my script. I read the lines to myself about Beatrice not wanting a husband with a beard. Leonato then tells her she could find a husband without a beard. But Beatrice always finds a way around a solution—she's like a lawyer finding loopholes. "Check it out," I say to Kyanna. "William Shakespeare is so cool." I keep reading. "He that hath a beard is more than a youth, and he that hath no beard is less than a man: and he that is more than a youth is not for me, and he that is less than a man, I am not for him . . ."

Kyanna nods. "It's like Beatrice just doesn't want to admit to it."

I stand up, stretching. "To what?"

Kyanna looks up at me. "To wanting anything."

"And why is that, do you think?" I ask, taking the stupid romance quiz from Kyanna's hands as she taunts me with it.

"Because," Kyanna says, snagging the quiz back and knocking me into my chair so we can get back to filling it out. "She might not get it."

18

I'M A MAN

AARON

Well, I mean, I am nearly eighteen. So legally speaking, I am a man. Almost.

And I did the stupid trapeze exercise without a bunch of whining and complaining, unlike a certain ex-diva I could name.

A certain ex-diva I'm not currently speaking to unless Shakespeare is supplying the words.

Things between us have been pretty frosty since she told me I was a little boy, but I guess it's good for our performances—Flannery actually said, "Okay, that didn't suck," after our rehearsal the other day. Which is pretty much the equivalent of a Tony nomination from anyone else.

Still, Charlie's gotten inside my head. Because what does it mean to be a man, really?

One day I'm sitting at lunch reading some manly detective novel when Kyanna approaches me. "Hey, bookworm," she says. "I need some exercise before my four o'clock call. My trusty phone tells me there's a place that rents mountain bikes about ten miles away. You feel like giving me a ride?"

Do I feel like giving Kyanna a ride? I suppose a grown man wouldn't so much as arch an eyebrow at the double entendre, so I close my book and say, "Sure."

We climb into the sweet generic American sedan that I (okay, my people) rented for the entire time we're here, and I plug the bike rental address into the GPS. As we rumble down the gravel road out of the compound, I spot Charlie looking quizzically at us. Good. Let her wonder.

As for me, I'm wondering how to approach a girl now that I can do it without having to keep it secret. And now that they're not really throwing themselves at me.

"I'm not gay," comes out of my mouth before I know what's happened.

"Uh, okay . . . ," Kyanna says, chuckling. "That was kind of random."

"Well, I mean, there is a train of thought. It's like, that whole thing was a misunderstanding, but to be honest, I didn't really care. But Charlie says all the women around here are going to feel all safe with me because they think I'm gay, and that I'm going to misunderstand that, and I mean, I don't—not that this is anything but a ride to the bike store—but I just wanted you to know up front that I'm a straight man, so, you know, don't think you can change clothes in front of me because I'm one of the girls kind of thing. You know?"

Kyanna laughs. "Not at all. Aaron, this— You don't think this is a date, do you?"

Well, no, but I kind of thought it might evolve into one. I'm so glad I have both the road and the GPS to look at. "Oh, God, not at all. I just . . . whatever. I just wanted you to know that I'm not gay."

"Message received."

"Turn left, fool!" the GPS barks at me, and Kyanna looks at it in amazement.

"Yeah, I paid extra to get the Mr. T voice on it," I say, grinning, and then I realize maybe that was kind of a non-grown-up move. I swear to God, Charlie is going to ruin everything for me. I stare at the road for a minute or so.

"So can I ask you something?"

"Okay," Kyanna says.

"And I really want you to be honest, okay? I'm not looking for reassurance here; I'm looking for honesty."

"Honest. I got it."

"Is my performance . . . Am I . . . Ah, well, Charlie and I had this big blowout, and she told me that I was still doing Jonah, that I couldn't find the character because Benedick is a grown-up."

I can feel my face getting hot. Falsely outed in the national press, not embarrassed at all. Admitting that something Charlie said got under my skin—yeah, I'm embarrassed by that.

"Well, I mean, I'm gonna have to sidestep the issue of

you—honestly, I'm a lot more worried about me. Because there's just not a lot there as far as Hero is concerned. Like, I feel like there's not a whole lot of character there, so I have to find it myself, but I'll do a horrible job. So in complete honesty, I'm not paying any attention to anybody else's performance. But I am reading the play a lot, and I don't agree that Benedick is a grown-up. I mean, yeah, he's a war hero and everything, but through most of the play, he's pretty much of a little kid. I mean, he's still kind of stuck in the 'girls are icky' stage."

"Hmmm . . . I guess I thought he was just faking that because he's in love with Beatrice."

"He's too dumb to know he's in love with Beatrice! He just thinks she drives him nuts."

"Well," I say, laughing, "if Benedick is clueless, I'm sure Charlie will feel like I've got a better shot at finding the character."

"Right turn, fool!" the GPS yells. I comply.

"Why do you care what she thinks, anyway?" Kyanna says.

"Oh, God, I don't care really. It's just that after four years of working together, and pretending to be in love was work, too—believe me, that was much harder work than the stupid show—she just knows exactly what buttons to push to get inside my head. It really . . . God, I honestly can't wait to be rid of her."

"Really?"

"Quit your jibber-jabber! Your destination is a hundred yards ahead on the left!" Mr. T informs us.

"Oh, yeah, really," I say.

"So why'd you come here?"

"Because I wanted to see if acting could be fun again. And because I guess I felt guilty about Charlie's career and what my alleged homosexuality had done to it, and I didn't want to let her down since they sold us to the festival as a package deal."

"I see. Well, you feel like renting a bike? I'll make sure to ride behind you so your very heterosexual eyes won't be drawn to my admittedly fabulous butt."

"Thanks, but I think I'm just gonna try to do some thinking."

"If you ask me, you do too much of that already," she says with a smile, then shuts her door and is gone.

"Where we goin'? Input a destination or shut me off!" Mr. T exclaims.

When I get back to my cabin after dropping off Kyanna, my phone, which has been sitting on my nightstand all day (I don't know what Flannery would do if my cell phone rang during rehearsal, but I'm pretty sure I would never be the same afterward), is ringing. Jo.

"Hey, Jo. I heard you shot your woman down," I say.

"You know, no one has ever made a 'Hey Joe' joke to me before. I congratulate you on your wit and originality!" Jo says.

"If I want someone to bust my balls, Charlie's cabin is just down the path from me."

"Well, don't worry, we'll have her moved next door. Or we'll move you. Anyway, you'll be next-door neighbors."

"What the hell are you talking about?"

"Well, if you ever answered your phone or checked your messages, you'd know what the hell I'm talking about. I've been pitching nonstop since you guys left, and I've finally sold your reality show."

"Reality show?"

"Yeah, you know, two big stars brought low and working at a rural Shakespeare festival. It's a great concept. And it'll really help you guys rehabilitate your image."

"Yeah. There's nothing like a reality show to stop you from being a laughingstock. Look at Paris Hilton. Or, no, bad example. Tori Spelling. No, okay, sorry, the Kardashians—no, Jack Osbourne. Spencer whoever the hell that guy is."

"Fielding."

"Aaron. My name is Aaron. Fielding is my stage name. And a stupid, pretentious one at that."

"No argument from me, but that's the brand I work for—"

"I'm not a brand!"

"No, *Aaron*, you're not a brand, but Fielding is. And this is what we need to do to protect the Fielding brand."

"I am not doing it. Absolutely not. I'm not having cameras up my ass every minute of the day here. I won't be able to act, and it'll make everyone hate us—"

"Yeah, struggling actors at a tiny regional Shakespeare festival really hate national TV exposure. What the hell was I thinking?"

"You don't— I don't care. I won't do it. I will not participate in this."

"I've been working nonstop on this for the last two weeks. I'm afraid I'm going to have to insist."

"No. Absolutely not. I will walk. I will leave Oregon and fly away the minute the cameras show up."

"I'm afraid that's not an option. You need to do what you're told on this."

"The hell I do. You're fired."

"No, I'm not."

"Yes, you are. I'll get my attorney to fax you all the relevant documents. As of right now, I don't have an agent."

Jo heaves a heavy sigh. "I'll be there this evening, and we'll—"

"No, Jo, don't come here. I don't want to—"

"Let's see—great, there's a flight in an hour and a half . . . I'll be at your cabin at seven thirty."

"No. Jo, no. Seriously, no. I do not—" I look at my screen. *Call ended*, it tells me.

. . .

I spend the rest of the day with my stomach in a knot. I do not want to see Jo. Ever again, really. Not just because I don't want Hollywood intruding on my Edenic Shakespeare experience, but also because I've been doing whatever Jo tells me to do for the last four years, and I'm afraid that once she's here I'll just give in to her and say yes, like I always do. I'm sure she's counting on the same thing.

The only thing I can do is to try to sabotage the reality show deal before she gets here. I come up with a plan, and when she gets back from her bike ride, Kyanna agrees to help me.

I don't mention anything to Charlie. This is partly because we're not really speaking right now, but it's also because I'm afraid of her talking me out of it, too.

I guess these are really baby steps toward becoming a man— avoiding all the women I usually obey—but they are steps.

I walk out of dinner as a Lexus SUV comes crunching up the gravel drive to the dining hall. Jo gets out. She's traded the usual power outfit for what appear to be brand-new outdoorsy L.L. Bean clothes.

"Fielding. Aaron. Whoever," she says. "Let's have a talk, shall we? I brought you something." She walks around to the back of the SUV and opens the hatch, revealing a seventeen-inch HDTV monitor, an Xbox 360, and a bunch of games. The kind of thing you'd use to buy off a teenage boy, and the kind of gift that wouldn't impress a man at all.

"Jo, I really don't— I'm enjoying the time I get to spend reading out here."

"Of course you are."

Now Charlie emerges from the dining hall and walks right over and shakes Jo's hand. "Hi! Jo, I spoke to Martinka earlier—I really want to thank you for all your hard work on this. I think it's going to be a great step."

"Thanks so much, Charlie—let's grab coffee when you get back."

"Sounds great," Charlie says as she trots off.

"You. Let's go to your cabin," Jo says, all trace of the smile she faked for Charlie disappearing from her face.

"Great," I say.

Once inside my cabin, Jo looks around, unable to disguise her distaste. "Well. They're certainly making you suffer for your art here, huh?"

"It's fine."

"That's great you think that. So listen, I brought the contracts. Have you had some time to cool down and rethink this?"

"No. I'm not doing it. And you're still fired."

"Stop that. You know only your mom can fire me, at least until you're eighteen. Now listen. I'm not going to lie to you. This isn't great money, and you're right, of course, about the whole reality show stigma, but it will keep you in the public eye. Especially because we've got a killer story arc planned."

"I thought it was a *reality* show."

"Don't be naive. You'll start out estranged from Charlie—we've arranged for James to do a guest shot on opening night, apologizing for not coming out and for falsely tagging you with the gay label—and then you'll move closer and closer to Charlie until the hang-gliding episode—"

"Hang gliding?"

"It's gonna be great TV, okay? And then you'll—"

"Well, I don't know, Jo. Lemme look at the contracts."

Jo's shoulders relax and her tight smile loosens up a little. "Great. I knew you'd see reason."

I flip through the contract. "Ooh. Morality clause."

"Same as the *J&J* contract."

"I'm afraid I might have violated this already."

"Listen, what happens in Oregon stays in Oregon, as long as the cameras aren't here."

"Well, you never know. I mean, with cell phone cameras everywhere, you can never tell exactly who's taking your picture. You should probably check the Internet just to make sure nothing's leaked out."

Jo looks at me and all pretense of a smile drops from her face. "What," she asks as she pulls her laptop from her bag and plugs the cell phone modem into the side of it. "Did. You. Do?"

Time passes as the page loads, and I really hope everything comes out okay.

"Oh, God, no," Jo says, staring slack-jawed at the laptop.

And there's the young Hollywood gossip site, featuring the photo of me, shirtless, with two other shirtless young men, heavy lidded, smiling, and holding a colossal smoking spliff in my hand.

"Wow. That looks kinda incriminating, huh?" I will never be able to thank Kyanna enough for this, since she provided the spliff—not actually full of marijuana because she didn't want to waste her stash if we weren't going to actually smoke it—and recruited the boy toys *and* took the photo. "Geez. Might be hard for a guy to get a job in family entertainment after that photo makes the rounds, huh?"

Jo is speechless.

"Well, Jo, will you please let me fire you now? I mean, I'm pretty sure Mom will make it official if you can ever get ahold of her."

"You ungrateful little—" Jo launches into a string of curses that are incredibly vivid even by her standards.

"I'll just give you a minute alone. See you!" I run along the path from my cabin, and it's all I can do not to skip with glee.

I guess I should formalize the end of my relationship with Jo, so I call Mom and leave her a voice mail asking her to fax Jo an official letter severing our relationship. But I realize that without Jo, I might have to figure out all kinds of stuff about my investments, the money I'm owed for *Jenna & Jonah* DVD sales, and all that stuff I never have to think about. I'm not ready to be that much of a man just yet. But I think I might know someone who is.

"Hey." Ryan answers on the first ring.

"Ryan. I have a— Hey, I have an idea. You want to work for me for a while? I just fired your boss. I don't need an agent, but I need somebody to take care of all the business stuff for a few months. I'll pay you whatever Jo pays you. No, you know what? I'll pay you ten percent more than Jo pays you. You make sure the real estate taxes are paid, meet with the accountants, stuff like that. I can't imagine it'll be as much work as you're doing now. How's that sound?"

"When do I start?"

"Right now. Just harass my mom until she agrees to fax a letter to Jo terminating her employment, voiding her power of attorney, stuff like that. And you can draw up a letter of understanding that you and Mom can sign and formalize our agreement. Okay?"

"Better than okay. Let me just back up my data and then I'm going to send Jo an e-mail and tell her where she can put her nonfat lattes."

"Awesome, Ryan. Thanks."

"Thank *you*, Aaron."

Aaron. I smile as I hang up the phone.

I guess I must be a little drunk with the excitement of taking charge of my own life, because I decide to go talk to Charlie.

I bound down the path to her cabin and knock on the door. She answers the door, BlackBerry plastered to her ear.

"Okay, Mart. Lemme call you back," she says and puts the phone down.

"Why?" she asks.

"I was afraid either you or Jo would talk me into this reality show nightmare, so I had to make it impossible for me to say yes."

"Great. Do you think you could have prepared me? Do you think maybe you could have talked to me about—"

"Charlie."

"Yeah?"

"That's not what a man would do. A man would take charge of his own life."

"A *man* takes the other people who depend on him into consideration when he makes a decision! A *man*—"

"The photo's genius, though, don't you think? Do you know I was actually smoking dried rosemary we lifted from the kitchen?"

"Do you know how much I care? Dammit, Aaron, I needed this show. We needed this show. It was our ticket back!"

"But I don't want to go back. I'm done. I keep telling everybody that, and nobody believes me. I'm done. You're going to have to get back without me."

"How could you? After all this time, how could you?"

"You know what? It was actually shockingly easy."

"You selfish—"

"No. Don't start with that. I've lived my whole life for the show, for the fauxmance, for the career, for the last four years. While most people are in high school having normal fun, I was working all the time. And I'm done. I'm not doing it anymore. You know why? Because I'm a grown-up, and I don't have to."

I turn and close the door to Charlie's cabin quietly as she begins some creative swearing of her own.

It's all I can do not to skip down the path to my cabin. I feel lighter and happier than I have in years.

Today I am a man.

✴19✴

ADVANCED EMOTIONS

CHARLIE

The fine print on my *Jenna & Jonah* contract was so explicit that there were only two flavors of ice cream I was allowed to consume in public. Vanilla "suggests purity and innocence" and strawberry "implies a fun spirit and youthful nature," so when Al invites me into town for gelato, the first thing I do is order against type. Or at least against my contract.

"I'll have caramel and deep chocolate," I say, leaning against the freezer and relishing the cool air.

"Living on the edge?" Al asks.

"Is caramel daring?" I ask with a smirk, wondering if chocolate is slutty or wistful, what *Celebrity Weekly* or *Gossip!* might say if they were to report my choice. But the beauty of it is, they aren't here. At least not yet. "It is sort of daring. I mean, per my contract I couldn't gain more than one pound, change my hair, or get any sort of piercing or tattoos. Caramel is about as daring as I can get."

Al takes his dish of pistachio outside, leading us to a small metal table on the sidewalk in the shade. The town center is close to the compound, and along with regular people, various costumed actors dash in for a quick gelato fix, careful not to stain their wardrobe.

"Tell me, Beatrice, what think you of this sweet?" Al asks, his body all relaxed but his voice as eloquent and deep as it is onstage.

I try to respond as Beatrice, but I don't know what to say so I just shrug. "Methinks it . . ." I fumble. "It's really good."

Al puts his spoon down and leans forward conspiratorially. "I declare I might never have seen a girl with ice cream seem so downtrodden."

I take another mouthful and sigh as a maiden in full Elizabethan regalia, save for her sneakers, walks by, savoring her cone as though she hasn't a care in the world. "It's just . . . how do you know when you're, actually, you know . . ."

"Acting?"

I nod. "When I watch you, or Kyanna, I'm totally caught up in the words and how convincing you are. Sometimes I have to remind myself you aren't actually your characters."

"Have you gotten to the advanced section of the book?"

I nod. "I even made the lists it told me to and whispered and yelled and made faces."

Al chuckles. "Maybe some of the book is drivel." Al continues to laugh, swooping his spoon into the green gelato and closing his eyes to the sun for a moment. "Acting is a lot like love. You know it only when you're in it. There's no doubt."

The cold gelato clashes with the heat from my blush. "Oh, well, maybe I'm just a loser in both . . ." Back in Season 2 of *Jenna & Jonah*, I sang a song called " 'Cause I'm (Un)Lucky in Love" in the pretend high school musical—very meta, because it also was a hit on the radio, at least in Eastern Europe. I had to intentionally act and sing badly because Jenna's rock star self is hidden from her high school class. So my costumes had to reflect the thrown-together nature of school plays, my timing was decent but not perfect, and I had to stumble over a line—at least in rehearsal—and everyone believed it. They actually thought I could be that bad. Sing off-key. Miss a line. Wear poly-blend clothing. It made me laugh, but it also made me feel bad for Jenna, or sort of for myself, like no one knew Jenna well enough to figure out her secret identity. I mean, come on, how convincing can a wig possibly be? Anyway, when it came time for the big night at Westfield High, Jenna wore the crappy costume and did a respectable job for a talented sophomore, but even though I'd planned on performing the song perfectly—out of spite for the producers and out of respect for myself—I unintentionally stumbled on the line "But when push comes to shove, I'm just unlucky in love." Ratings were great, but I was furious they wouldn't let me reshoot the scene. "It's so authentic," someone said when we stopped rolling. It was inauthentic in twelve different ways.

"How is what I'm doing now different from what I did before?" I lick my lips. "I mean, how do I know I'm not faking my way through a fake world in a fake way?"

Al shakes his head. "You saw the cast the other night after you rehearsed the final scene. Come on. Everyone was sucked in and completely at your mercy. Television history or no, you have *it*." He peers at me. "It. Onstage, it's all there." He finishes his gelato and clears his throat. "You know, when I played Sergeant Malloy—this was way before your time—I once had a scene with this woman . . . She was a criminal, a bank robber or a government spy—who can remember such details now? Anyway, I had to shoot her." He points to his chest. "Right here. Big network scandal, can a man really fire at a woman? Again, this was when you were a fetus."

I twist my hair back into a knot and lick every last bit of caramel and chocolate from my spoon, stopping short of sticking my face in the bowl. "So what happened? Did you do it?"

Al mimes pulling a gun from an imaginary holster. "We were filming live, okay? This was cutting-edge back then. And I pulled the gun out, fired at her, and the blood bag inside her shirt didn't explode—so, as you know, this means no gore. No real blood, no fake blood, no nothing. Cameras are rolling, so I do what all good actors do."

I lean forward, eager to hear his tricks of the trade. "What's that?"

"I improvised." He stands up so we can walk back to

rehearsal, where legions of actors—some better, some maybe worse—wait for me to perform.

"How'd you improvise—? I mean, obviously, I've done that a little, like on the show my line was 'How's it gonna look, Jonah?' and I said, 'How's it gonna seem, Jonah?'" The minute this is out of my mouth I start to laugh. Could that be lamer? I mean, one word? That's a substitution, not an improvisation!

"You've read the book, right?" Al wipes his forehead with his sleeve, heat reddening his face. "Advanced emotions. That's what it takes to improvise, because improvisation comes from instinct, not memorization. Your gut!" He pounds his own stomach. "Your gut's where the improv hides."

Al and I walk away from the sidewalk cafés and small shops, past the costume building with its wide porch, and toward the big main stage where we will be performing as the main attraction soon.

"I don't know what to do with the rest of my life," I say to Al.

Al nods as though I've just offered him a choice of donut. "Me neither. Maybe I'll hawk undergarments for the elderly. Maybe I'll star in a new film about an aging baseball coach who finds his long-lost son."

"Really?"

Al nods, his white hair flopping in the wind. "It's called *Finding Home*—it's not bad, really."

"And the diapers for old folks?"

Al grins. "The pay's not bad and I get a lifetime supply of them!"

I smile at him, feeling for the first time a sense of how much I'll miss him, miss this—the cast as family. Even when the director yells at me, it feels okay, like a sibling or scary aunt shouting for my best interest. "I'm sorry I won't get to do this again," I say when we're outside the theater. "Stage always seemed so small when I was on TV, but being here—it's weird. Suddenly that tiny screen—even though it's in all those houses—feels more remote."

"Maybe that's why they call it a remote control," Al says as we wave to Kyanna, who is heading inside with a silent Aaron next to her. He doesn't even look my way.

And maybe it's true, that I've been controlled by remote, by contracts, right down to what I'm allowed to eat or wear or say or who to share my days with. I glare at Aaron as he slams the front door. "Subtle, Aaron, really." I kick the ground and puffs of dirt go into the air, sending a wave of grime over my flip-flops. How dare Aaron decide for me, for us both, the future of the reality show? How dare he put his foot down when it stomps on mine?

"He's a dimwit," I say, my pulse racing, even though my heart beats double-time just thinking about his mouth. "Everything about him makes me want to slap him. To shove him and demand an apology . . . for ruining everything, or changing it."

"Who?"

I shake my hair free of its knot. "Benedick—Aaron, I mean. He's so . . . so . . . He's a weasel."

"Even a weasel needs understanding and compassion."

"Don't defend him! He's undefendable." I pause. "Indefensible? Whatever. The point is, he has such a high opinion of himself, but he doesn't even want to admit who he is, where he comes from. At least I acknowledge my bizarre upbringing. I don't hide my past from the viewers . . ." My cheeks redden as I think about the way Aaron's fingers felt laced in mine.

"What about your future?" Al asks. "And what about the past you had with Aaron?"

"He wasn't Aaron. He was Fielding." I pause, thinking back. "You know what's so weird? When we first started, way back before the show took off and we started pretending, we were starting to get really close." I bite my lip, remembering. "We could've been . . ."

"Good friends?"

I think back to the diner where we used to eat late at night or at four in the morning before our call, just us, orange juice, and French toast—I took the crusts and gave him the mushy middles—and we'd make up inappropriate songs or share our latest complaints about agents, or just quote our favorite movie lines. "More than that." Inside, I feel a clenching. My stomach churns and my throat tightens. My eyes sting but don't fill. "It's like I'm losing . . ." I pause, take a breath. "Like I've lost my friend and my job."

Al pats my back. "And what have you gained?"

I don't answer. I just watch Al go down the steps toward a woman I don't know. "It's instinct, Charlie," he calls up. "Your mind and heart will take over—on stage and off." He hugs the woman and then comes back to me to explain. "By the way, that scene? I shot her, nothing happened, the script guy's having a coronary, the director is mouthing, 'Stab her, stab her'—not that I had a knife."

The feeling that I might actually cry disappears. "So what'd you do?"

"I grabbed her, looked her in the eyes, and kissed her." He smiles and looks at the woman he hugged and motions for her to come over. "Highest ratings ever . . . but more importantly, I got an Emmy out of it. You know why?"

I shrug. "People like romance?"

"People schmeople." He takes the woman's hands in his. "They didn't care that I never shot her. Didn't care that it wasn't the most sensible thing for Sergeant Malloy. I did what I felt. That's acting. That's living it. That's real. You're acting real stuff, not fake. Beatrice cannot admit to herself how much she really loves Benedick, so she convinces herself that she loathes him. It's the other side of the coin and it's safe. What happens when both sides meet?"

I stand there, feeling everything at once: rage that I would have to do yet another stupid show that will typecast me not only as the star who failed, but the star who failed alone, and annoyance that my instinct was to say yes to the show as though I had no other option, while Aaron did what he wanted. Maybe that says something about him. Maybe he's more of a whole person, a man, than I gave him credit for. As I fume and seethe, Al hugs the woman. She tells me her name is Gertrude Wilck, which sounds familiar, but I don't know why. She has a long rope of silver blond hair tied in a loose ponytail and an ankle-length denim skirt. They hug. Al says something to her. She studies me and Al says, "This is the girl."

I furrow my brow. "The girl . . . ?"

"He shot me," the woman says. "In a manner of speaking."

There are no bullet wounds, but I know what Al means. I leave them to their reunion, amazed that one split-second decision could change their lives. What if the blood had exploded? Would he have kissed her anyway? How do you know when to act on your instinct and when to muffle the inner voice? What happens when the script is learned but there's more to figure out?

20

SHE LOVES YOU (YEAH, YEAH, YEAH)

AARON

I'm scared, of course.

After *Much Ado About Nothing* closes, I have no idea what I'm going to do. This is because I have no one telling me what to do. At first it was cool, feeling completely free for the first time in my life, but freedom is freaking scary. If there were something I *had* to do, well, that would take away the responsibility for figuring out how to build a life I can both enjoy and be proud of.

Then I'd have someone else to blame if I was unhappy. This "being a man" business kind of sucks.

I try to bring this up with Kyanna one Saturday at lunch.

"I mean, I just— It's intimidating, you know, trying to figure out what to do with the rest of my life."

"Yeah, must be tough to have so much money that you can go anywhere and do anything without having to worry about how you're going to eat. I just have to hope the restaurant is holding my job for me like they promised they would, and that my landlord is going to replace the broken windowpane before winter comes. Your existential angst really moves me."

"Ah. Yeah. I guess I can see how it would."

"Honestly, Aaron. Get your head out of your butt. You've got what most people dream of. Let yourself enjoy it."

"I know, I know. You're right. I guess everything just feels off right now. Charlie—"

"Is going to land on her feet, and you're not responsible for her."

"I guess . . . it's weird. I feel guilty about leaving her behind."

"I'm thinking a few weeks in Bermuda might cure you of that. Listen, I gotta go. I've been, uh, burning the midnight oil"—there's that pot-smoking pantomime again—"until really late every night, and I need a nap so Flannery doesn't hand me my ass this afternoon."

"Okay. I'll see you later."

Honestly, the one person I could really talk to about this is the person I'm not currently speaking to. I mean, I know Kyanna's right, but nothing is ever simple, and living the dream has been kind of a nightmare. Charlie would get that. But she'd pretend not to, just to piss me off. If she were speaking to me.

I go back to my cabin and look at the schedule. After tonight's run-through, we've got a full tech rehearsal at eight in the morning. I have no idea why, unless it's just to torture us. Kyanna told me that the first tech rehearsal is a nightmare—lots of standing around the stage while the crew tries to get the lighting cues right. "It's guaranteed to be the most grueling, boring time you will ever spend on a stage," Kyanna said.

And then Sunday afternoon is our last real break until the festival closes. Full dress rehearsals every afternoon, plus to-be-determined work on parts that need extra work, as decreed by Flannery. And then Friday we open and run in repertory for two weeks. And then the first day of the rest of my life.

Well, what's the point of having money if you're not going to enjoy it? I call Ryan and ask him if he will set up a plan for me.

The run-through is god-awful. Everyone in the cast is forgetting lines and just giving basically horrible performances. Charlie and I are especially out of sync, which of course makes our scenes suck. I have to say that being entangled all the time did help us in our acting—on the show, there was trust and communication between us that made acting with her really easy. Now I have no idea what she's thinking at any given time, and though we can recite our lines and hit our marks, it just isn't working.

After the rehearsal, Flannery gathers the cast, and we sit

in a circle, metaphorical tails between our legs, awaiting the verbal thrashing we all know we deserve.

"Apparently"—Flannery is whispering rather than yelling, which is twice as terrifying—"I was misled. I was told that I would be working with professional actors here. I would be embarrassed to mount this production at a community theater that performs at the Elks Lodge. At a festival like this, it's simply unthinkable.

"None of you seem to care much about embarrassing yourselves, so I will just ask you not to humiliate me when we open on Friday. None of us will be back next summer, and all of us, *all of us*"—the repetition is accompanied by a special glare aimed at Charlie and me—"will have a very hard time finding any employment at all in this profession once the stink of this production wafts across the theatrical world. Now get out and get it together."

We all slink away, and I find myself walking next to Charlie. "Well, that was brutal," I say.

"Oh, why the hell do you care?" she asks. "You're retiring anyway, right? Soon you'll be far away from all of this and all of us, and you won't have to worry if we're not employed. You'll be fine." She walks away from me, and I really want to run after her and tell her it's not like that, I do care, I am a professional, and she and I need to get ourselves right before Friday night so that we can do work we're proud of.

Instead I kick the wall.

"Easy there," I hear Kyanna saying from behind me. "You're gonna need that foot to work for at least two more weeks."

"Yeah," I say, embarrassed to have been caught in a temper tantrum. "It's just that she makes me nuts."

"Oh, don't worry about her," she says. "First run-throughs always suck and directors always ream you out afterward. She'll be tearing the tech crew a new one tomorrow."

"Oh. Flannery. Yeah. I guess I'm not too worried about her."

"I see. Well, no more kicking, okay?"

"All right."

I head back to my cabin and don't kick anything else. It takes me a long time to fall asleep, because things I wish I had said to Charlie keep rattling around in my brain.

On any two-camera sitcom, the crew can light the three main sets in their sleep (in *Jenna & Jonah*'s case, that would be Beach House, High School Classroom, and Rehearsal Studio), and any adjustment that needs to be done to the lights is done with stand-ins while the stars sit in their dressing rooms drinking imported mineral water.

In a low-budget, small-scale theatrical production, though, everybody stands on the stage and crawls through the play one line at a time while, apparently, the director threatens bodily harm to the crew if they keep screwing up. At least that's what happens to us on Sunday morning.

I find Charlie backstage while Edgar is onstage and

Flannery is making the lighting crew run through their cues again and again and again.

"Hey," I say.

"I'm sorry," Charlie says. "I'm just trying to stay in the moment here, and I really can't have any distractions during a performance. You understand."

"Dammit, Chuck, cut it out. Can I just talk to you?"

"One, don't call me Chuck. Two, Charlie's not here, and Beatrice doesn't speak backstage."

"We need to talk this out and get ourselves right."

"We need no such thing. Soon you'll be away from me and this, free at last, and you needn't give it a thought. We're professionals and will deliver a great performance. Now I really must insist that you stop speaking to me."

I walk away and take deep breaths and try not to kick anything.

After the tech rehearsal ends at last, I try to forget Charlie and focus on having some fun. Flannery dismisses us so she can tear into the tech crew some more, and before everyone departs I yell out, "Hey, everybody, can I just have your attention for a sec?"

Most people stop and look at me. "We've got a really busy couple of weeks coming up, so I thought we should have some fun this afternoon. Nobody has to come or anything, but I hope you guys will help me enjoy some of my ex–TV star money. Walk outside and you'll see what I mean."

Outside the theater is a big bus, or if you believe the words painted on the side, LUXURY COACH. The door opens and the driver hands me a duffel bag.

"Okay, kid," Al yells out, "what's going on?"

"Well," I say, reaching into the bag, "here's a hint."

I open the duffel bag and start throwing baseball caps out to the cast. The black caps feature a jaunty cartoon beaver poking his head through the middle of a big white capital *P*.

Most people look at the caps quizzically, so I have to say, "This bus is bound for PGE Park, home of the Portland Beavers, where I've hired a luxury box for us to enjoy tonight's game versus the Albuquerque Isotopes. There will be abundant vegan treats for me and those who are similarly inclined, and plenty of dead-animals-in-tube-shape for those of you who enjoy that kind of thing."

The entire cast cheers, and I feel like Santa Claus.

MUCH ADO ABOUT NOTHING, the sign on our luxury suite reads. We enter and find the vegan and omnivorous catering options clearly labeled, abundant beverages, and, outside, a beautiful night for baseball.

I load a plate full of Ma Po tofu and mustard greens, grab a seltzer, and head out to a seat under the lights. I think about how Kyanna was right—I am really lucky to have enough money to do something like this, and right now, watching a baseball game with good food in front of me, life is good.

So why don't I feel happy?

Most of the cast remains in the luxury suite, while only a few come out to actually watch the game. I'm pleasantly surprised when Kyanna comes to sit next to me.

"Hey, thank you," I say.

"What for?" she asks.

"For what you said yesterday. It made me think about enjoying my money and, you know, sharing the wealth with my beloved castmates."

"Happy to help. Especially when there's free food in it for me. You pretty much can't go wrong with free food and actors. The first trays were picked clean in about thirty seconds—even the vegan crap."

"It's not crap! This is top-notch Chinese food! It's not like some nutritional yeast nut loaf or something!"

"Whatever. The point is, people are happy. This is a good stress reliever. Thanks."

"My pleasure. Beavers are up two to nothing, you know."

"Whatever again. I just wanted to thank you. Are you feeling any better?"

"Yeah," I lie. "I'm feeling a lot better."

Kyanna gives me a long look. Maybe my acting wasn't especially convincing. "Glad to hear it. I'll see you a little later."

She walks up the aisle back to the suite, and though the Isotopes' cleanup hitter is facing down a 3–2 count with men on first and second, I turn away from the action to watch

Kyanna's butt as she walks up the stairs. At the top of the steps, she stops for a second and says something to Al, who smiles. They give each other a high five.

I turn back and find I've missed an inning-ending double play. I put my feet up on the railing and soon find Al sitting next to me.

"Hey, kid," he says. "What's the score?"

"Beavers two, 'Topes zero."

"Do you follow a lot of minor-league ball?"

"Tonight I do," I say, smiling.

Al takes a long pull on his Big Gulp–sized beer. "Ah. This is good stuff, kid, thanks."

"My pleasure."

"Listen, Aaron. I've gotta ask you something," Al says. I look over at him, and his eyes are on the game.

"Okay."

"So you know I've been kind of mentoring Charlie, right?"

"Yeah."

"So she's got a problem right now, and I'm afraid it's affecting her performance. I like the kid, and I want her to get good notices when we go up—and I know she can—but right now she's got this distraction that I'm afraid is hurting things."

"I just couldn't do the reality show, Al. I mean, I wish her luck in her career—I really do—it's just—"

"This isn't a career thing. You know that. Charlie's a

professional. She'd never let job concerns affect her performance."

"So what is it?"

"It's the fact that she's madly in love with someone."

I take a second to chew on this as the Beavers' center fielder flies out to the second baseman. "Hmm. Who's the lucky guy?"

"I'm sitting next to him."

"Bullshit."

"I shit you not. She told me. And I don't mean told me like I read her body language or something. We were talking about what's going on with her performance, and she said she feels like she can't really let herself get into the performance because she knows she's losing you in two weeks, and it's just too painful to let herself fully inhabit the part of someone who's in love with you."

"Well. I— She acts like— I mean, she's been kind of acting pissed at me all the time . . ."

"Of course she's pissed at you! She thinks you're rejecting her!"

"It's not . . . I'm not . . . I just . . ."

"Listen, kid, it's really none of my business anyway. But if you can find a way to fix this by opening night, I think it's going to help us all. Now, if you'll excuse me, there's a plate of nachos up there with my name on it."

I watch the rest of the game without taking it in at all.

People come and sit by me for half an inning or so and I try to make conversation, but my brain is a million miles away.

Charlie's in love with me?

It certainly explains a lot. It also gives me a whole lot to think about.

On the bus back to the festival grounds, I keep sneaking peeks at Charlie, and twice I catch her sneaking peeks at me. It's no wonder she's pissed. Charlie's the ultimate control freak, and love is something that makes you completely out of control.

Something that makes you, for example, lie awake in your cabin thinking, trying to make all the data fit with the new evidence. Maybe she sees my rejection of the show as a rejection of her. Which it is. Or was. Only not really. It was about something else. I think.

And then there's me. How do I feel? If Charlie really is in love with me, can I reciprocate without just becoming part of someone else's plans again? But this isn't part of her plan, which is probably why she's so upset. And it's certainly not part of my plan. But I don't know if I have a choice about whether to reciprocate. I kind of have to evaluate my own recent behavior against the possibility that my feelings for Charlie might not be the same ones I always thought they were.

My thoughts keep going around in circles, which is completely exhausting. So why does it keep me up half the night?

And then there's this, the next day: Act 2, Scene 1 on Monday's dress rehearsal. Charlie's costume prominently features her most prominent feature, the globes of glory that led to a hundred Web sites posting countdown clocks to her eighteenth birthday. And she changes up her performance just enough to make me wonder.

"I cannot endure my Lady Tongue," I spit in Beatrice's direction as she enters stage right while I'm exiting stage left.

"Come, lady, come; you have lost the heart of Signior Benedick," Don Pedro says to Beatrice.

"Indeed," she says, and though I'm standing offstage and she's supposed to be staring wistfully after me, she pauses, meets my eyes, and says this: "Indeed, my lord, he lent it me awhile; and I gave him use for it—a double heart for a single one."

Then she takes a beat and turns back to Don Pedro. It's clear to me that Al's right. Charlie is in love with me. And maybe she always has been.

I've been a complete idiot. But at least now I know why my plan to be a lazy, rich young adult or possibly a lazy, rich college student left me feeling empty. Because she's completely infuriating, she drives me crazy, and I don't know what the hell I would do without her. Without Charlie in the plan, it's never been enough. Maybe it never will be.

21

LOVE SOUGHT

CHARLIE

"I can't breathe," Kyanna says, clutching her stomach.

Backstage, a whirlwind of activity. Al dusting his face with powder; a makeup person putting finishing touches on eyebrows, slicking them with thick, waxy paste so they show up under the glare of the house lights; actors running through lines or warm-ups; and Kyanna mending her own shoe, a high-heeled boot, actually, whose button popped off. I pull Kyanna up to a standing position and she's still grabbing her waist.

"Look, women wore these every day, so quit moaning," I tell her and try to stand up straight to maximize every inch of breathing space in the ridiculously tight corset. "We can handle this." My makeup is worse than on *Jenna & Jonah*, thick enough to stand up on its own, with eye shadow bright enough that it's probably visible from space. I keep thinking about this song Aaron and I sang a cappella under the bleachers in Season 1, before everything got out of control on set and off: "When you seek love, it finds you, open your eyes—it won't blind you. Love sought, never bought. Love sought." We used to mock it, rhyming "overwrought" with "sought." But now it's not the lyrics I'm thinking of. It's the way we hung out under the bleachers after the filming stopped. It's the way we ate dinner together in Carpinteria. It's the way I realize I've been looking for one thing—fame—when what I've really wanted has been next to me for so many seasons.

"Speak for yourself." Kyanna shakes her head. "I'll never be tough enough for corsets."

"You know what they say in Hollywood." I shrug. Kyanna gives me her "no, I really don't" look, all cocky with her hip thrust out. "If you want a Golden Globe, you've gotta wear a corset."

"Or have an accent," she adds in an unidentifiable one.

I nod. "Take slow, shallow breaths." My floor-length gown is deep rose trimmed in midnight blue silk, with slightly poufed sleeves and enough cleavage revealed so no one mistakes me for a boy, like in the production of *Twelfth Night* we saw yesterday in the outdoor space. There are lots of other plays going on at the festival and it's been refreshing to see so many actors put themselves out there for rejection or praise.

I keep thinking about that performance, about pretending to be someone other than who you really are, to disguise your feelings, to find out other people's feelings, to mask love. Love sought is good, but given unsought is better. That's the line I repeated over and over as I tried to fall asleep last night. Outside was a party, the revelry that announced the show goes up today. Since some of the people will stay on and some will leave, this is the beginning of the end—so this will serve as a wrap party, too. In some ways, I'm ready. I know the part, I have the lines down, the outfits are pressed and fitted, our blocking is finished. But in other ways, I know I'm not at all prepared for the ending of this, because it's really the ending of so much more. All the work we've put into this, that I have put into my role, makes me sure I'm on another level in terms of acting. But then what's next?

"Did you see *Twelfth Night?*" I ask Kyanna.

"It was set in the 1920s, right?"

I nod. "Great Depression. Hats. Suits. Ankle boots with buttons. But it worked."

"It's funny how many of Shakespeare's plays focused on mistaken identity," Kyanna says. "This one class I took back in the city was all about how those mix-ups allowed the characters to be themselves."

"Like you're more you as someone else?" I ask, and then it hits me. All that time I was pretending to be Jenna, part of me was there, and another part grew attached to my costar. And it wasn't all bad, despite what Aaron thinks. And when we were in Carpinteria, that was another side of me. "Did you ever think that maybe you're not just one simple person? That maybe there are lots of you?"

206

Kyanna doesn't make a joke or laugh; she just regards me in the mirror. "Different versions of the same self."

"Exactly," I say.

Al, who has been eavesdropping a bit, approaches us before he takes his place on the other side of the stage. "You didn't read that book all the way through, did you?" I shake my head. "If you had, you'd have read this line: 'Only when we accept that our true selves and our character selves are one, and they comprise multiple layers of the same person, will we be great onstage. To act is to admit to more than one reality.' "

Tears spring into my eyes and though I'm surprised by them—I am human after all!—I will myself not to ruin the acres of makeup applied to my skin. So much time and effort has been put into this. I honestly don't think I've worked as hard on anything in my life. I tell that to Kyanna and she nods, facing me in her gown, which is three tiered and makes a swooshing sound as she spins me around in a pretheater show of excitement and nerves.

"But I think there's something else you have worked on just as much," she says, joining her hands in mine.

I think about this while practicing my curtsy, gracefully pulling one leg behind me and keeping eye contact while bending down. "I'm not sure I know what you mean."

"Oh, fair lady," she says in an accent no one would know isn't authentic. "Surely you can delve into the past and present and conjure the reality of thy hardest work."

"A hint would be good here."

"What thou workest hardest at is the same thing as that which thou needest most."

"A job. Exactly."

Kyanna shakes her head, sending a little errant braid down from the careful pile on her head. I go over to help her pin it up. "Think again. Or rather, don't think, feel. That which thou workest hardest at is the same which angers thee the most."

Anger. Work. "Ah, methinks understanding hast come to find me." I check my eye makeup in the mirror. "Just to clarify, yes, Aaron took an inordinate amount of work. And he infuriates me like no other." I clear my throat. "But that's as far as it goes."

Kyanna nods slowly, deliberately. "Yeah, that's what I told him you'd say."

I whip around. "What? What do you mean you figured that's what I'd say? When did you guys speak about this?"

Kyanna shakes her head, going to the mirror to reapply her lip gloss. "At the baseball game the other day . . . and that night at rehearsal . . . but never mind. It's no big deal."

I twist the gloss right from her hand. I may be dressed as a maiden, but the costume doesn't hide my character's pluck. "Stop. Go back. From the beginning."

Kyanna takes my stage direction, practicing her dance moves as she does, elaborately twisting and pirouetting as she explains. "So he—the gentleman in question—pulls me aside and does what any true annoyed person must do. Confess. He leans in and says, whispering in my ear with breath that, I might add, did speak well of his vegan lifestyle in that it reeked neither of hot dog nor salami but of mint. He says—"

"We have six minutes before I either go and make an idiot of myself or shine, Kyanna. Out with it," I say, hoping I can keep my lines straight with all this new info being poured into my brain.

"The long and the short of it—mainly the long—is that he doth protest too much."

"In English. Real English, not theater-in-the-round stuff."

Kyanna tilts her head and lays it on me. "Dude, the guy's crazy about you." She waits for my reaction, but I have none. "He. Loves. You."

"Benedick, you mean?"

Kyanna nods and my spirits sink. But why would they sink if I don't care myself? Of course Benedick loves me. My character. That's how the play works. Then Kyanna says, "Benedick *and* Aaron. They're one and the same in this matter."

He loves me? Benedick? Fielding Withers? Aaron? He—they—love me?

"Two minutes, Charlie," the stagehand, a shadow in black, whispers. My throat is dry, but my heart flickers like the lights at intermission. He loves me? I can't help but smile, a real smile, a full smile. Kyanna takes her place and I ready

209

myself. Out there, somewhere, is everything that comes next, on camera or stage and off, but where does Aaron fit into the picture?

The house lights are dark. Only the stage is illuminated. Well, the stage and me. If he loves me, then what do I do? And what does it mean? Love sought is good; love unsought is better. We never asked for love, did we? Now, in my corset, with my heart tight against my rib cage and my future in front of me, I'm the one who can't breathe.

22

TEAR THE ROOF OFF THE SUCKA

AARON

I'm more nervous than I have ever been in my life. Years ago, when they flew me from Cincinnati to LA for the final call-back for *Jenna & Jonah*, I didn't sleep for two days. And then nailed the audition. Now I haven't slept in two days *and* my stomach has rejected pretty much everything I've tried to eat.

It's not the play. It's really not. I know we'll be playing to a full house, and most of the people in the audience will be there waiting for us to fall on our asses, hoping to be the first ones to e-mail Perez and tell him how much we suck. And there will probably be a few industry types there, maybe not hoping to trumpet our failure all over the Internet, but just gawking at the horror of our performances like rubber-neckers staring at a wreck on the I-10 at rush hour.

And we're going to disappoint them all by not sucking. We're going to smack them upside the head with some iambic

211

pentameter and make them thank us for it. Rehearsals this week have run the gamut from competent to brilliant, so when I say I'm not worried about the show, I really mean it.

I really thought I was going to have to address Charlie's apparent love for me before the show if, like Al said, it was going to affect her performance. But it looks like Charlie has finally hit her stride, and she's been getting better and more confident with every rehearsal.

Which is good, because I couldn't figure out what I would say. "I will always treasure our friendship, but, as Vanessa so memorably sang in *High School Musical 2*, I gotta go my own way." Or possibly, "I think maybe I have similar-type feelings, but if we've learned anything from the last four years, it should be that it would never work between us." Or possibly, "I love you, too."

That's the scariest one, and when I rehearse these things in my head, that's the one that feels the truest. Which is why I've been barfing so much.

I *cannot* be in love with Charlie. It's simply not in the plan. Not that I really had a detailed plan in place, but the one thing I felt sure of was that I was getting off the Hollywood merry-go-round.

Two days after the baseball game, Ryan called me to tell me that he'd secured me an apartment in lower Manhattan at a ridiculous bargain price. (For Manhattan. My one-bedroom apartment in Manhattan cost me about what a ten-bedroom house in Cincinnati might.) It's too late for me to get into NYU or Columbia for the fall semester, of course, but maybe I can just live in peace and relative anonymity for a while.

I can't enter into some kind of bicoastal romance. And, anyway, I've been pretending with Charlie for the last four years, and I am ready to play the field for a while. I am not in love with Charlie. I'm not.

That's what I tell myself. But my stomach is apparently not convinced.

Dammit.

There was an episode about this, of course. Season 1, Episode 20, when it wasn't clear whether we'd be picked up for Season 2, and the writers figured they should have friends/next-door neighbors/bandmates Jenna and Jonah admit their love for each other just so the kids who loyally watched the first season wouldn't feel cheated if it never came back.

It is, in my opinion, the best episode of the show. Maybe because the writers figured they had nothing to lose, they made an episode that was just as corny as the other nineteen but which was, according to the fans, genuinely touching, too.

"You know she likes you," Hunter Davenport, who played my dorky asthmatic sidekick Nebs ('cause he had such bad asthma as a kid that his baby sister thought his name was Nebulizer—because what's funnier than childhood asthma!) said as we pretended to play video games, staring at a non-existent screen that was actually the camera lens.

"Well, of course she likes me, Nebs," I replied. "We've been friends for, like, ever. I like her, too!"

"No, dummy. I mean she *likes* you likes you."

I dropped my controller and hopped off the couch, and Nebs continued. "Did you see the way she was staring at that girl who was hanging around you after the concert last night?"

"Not really."

"Well, it was the same way she looked at me when I broke her Barbie dream house in fourth grade," Nebs said.

I bugged my eyes out. Big laugh. Shaking, I went to the fridge and poured myself a soda to calm my nerves.

"And you know what else?" Nebs said. "You like her, too. Like that. Yes, you do."

Spit take—I sprayed soda all over the kitchen. We had to work on that for an hour before I could get the proper volume and coverage from my spat soda. Long pause for laughter. They actually had to cut some of the laughter when they aired the show, because I had managed to spit soda on the then-president of the network, who was standing just off camera, and the audience roared as he flapped his silk tie around, trying to shake the soda drops off.

"You are crazy, Nebs," I said.

"Am I? Then why were you going to fight Jimmy Bonasoro?"

"He said I couldn't play guitar!"

"And it had nothing to do with him taking Jenna out for ice cream?"

"That . . . that was a coincidence!" I stammered.

"If you think about it, you'll see that I'm right," Nebs said.

Cue montage! Our song "Maybe You're the One," slow, pretty, and featuring a harmony so sweet it should come with an insulin shot, played as a montage of shots from the past nineteen episodes flashed past—us laughing together, me looking jealous as Jenna and Jimmy eat ice cream, Jenna looking jealous as Candy hangs around the stage after the concert, and the time we got locked in a supply closet backstage and almost kissed.

Back to the beach house. I was still standing in the kitchen, slack-jawed. Nebs walked in, wearing different clothes than the last time we saw him. "Whoa, dude, when I told you to think about it, I didn't mean you should stand there all night!" Big laughs.

Two scenes later, Jenna and Jonah found themselves backstage and locked in a dressing room courtesy of their wisecracking unattractive best friends.

"Jenna," I said. "Don't quit the band."

"Why not?" Jenna spat back. "I'm dead weight, remember? Just the pretty girl singer who can't play an instrument."

"I'm sorry, Jenna. You know I didn't mean that."

"And, anyway, I think this band is ruining our friendship. I mean, we've been friends since kindergarten, Jonah, and I don't want to lose that. I'm afraid the band is changing things."

"I don't think it's the band that's changing things," I muttered.

"What do you mean?" Jenna answered, looking both confused and hopeful.

"I mean, we're ruining our friendship because . . . because I think . . . because I want to be more than friends, okay?"

Jenna looks at the ground. She looks up, and she's laughing.

"Yeah," I say, terror in my eyes. "I was just— I mean, we've been friends for so long I guess it would be kind of funny—"

"No, dummy! I'm just laughing because I thought you'd never get it! No offense, Jonah, but you are pretty slow sometimes. I was afraid I was going to have to literally hit you over the head for you to recognize what's been going on between us!"

"You mean . . . you, too?"

"Of course, goofy. Listen, if we're going to ruin our friendship, I'd much rather ruin it this way than with a stupid fight."

"Cool. Me, too."

"So are you gonna stand there all day, or are you gonna kiss me?"

So I did. Cue the up-tempo, hard-rockin' reprise of "Maybe You're the One" and roll the credits.

That episode has been the blueprint for how real romance begins for an entire generation of teens and, yeah, I guess I have to include myself in that. But when I play my own montage, I don't edit the bad stuff. And Charlie and I don't have much of a friendship to ruin. And nobody's going to write the lines for me. Oh, yeah, and I don't know in advance how it's all going to turn out. I mean, you get the main characters on a teen show together, you know nothing bad's ever going to happen. They're not going to cheat on each other, or grow apart, or ever face any problems more serious than wacky schemes gone awry, unless the producers decide they need a Very Special Episode.

But in real life, you don't know how it's going to work out. You don't know how the other person is going to respond, and you don't know if you're going to say the wrong thing and ruin everything, and sometimes you don't even really know what the hell you want.

Opening night. I managed to keep down a papaya smoothie this morning, so I may actually have enough energy to give a competent performance. The house is filling up slowly, and we're peeking out from backstage just like I did in middle school.

Ten minutes later, Flannery calls us all together in the greenroom. It's a tight squeeze. She climbs on a table in the middle of the room and says this:

"Actors. Watching this production go from the hell of our first run-through to the last two dress rehearsals, which were brilliant—if flawed, and I know you're all remembering my notes—well, this is one of those experiences that makes me proud to be here, proud to be a director, proud to have devoted my life to a craft that is often cruel, rarely remunerative, present company excepted"—she looks at Charlie and then me, and everybody laughs, including us—"and always uncertain. I'm proud of you, I'm proud of us, and our audience is going to thrill to what you do here tonight. Good show," she says quietly.

"Good show," the cast answers, slightly louder.

"Good show," Flannery says, yelling now.

"Good show!" we answer back.

"GOOD SHOW!" Flannery screams.

"GOOD SHOW!" we scream back.

I catch Charlie's eye across the room. I nod and smile. She, for what feels like the first time in weeks, smiles back at me. My pulse quickens, and my stomach, a cold, hard knot all week, suddenly feels warm and relaxed.

Actors talk about becoming the character, but you never really become the character. At least I don't. What I become is a guy who's watching from the very back of my brain as the character inhabits my body and uses my voice. Which is to say I never really go away and let the character take over. I'm always there, in the back of my head.

And sometimes I sneak into the front of my head. Like when I'm masked in the Act 2 party, spinning Charlie around the dance floor, I'm trying hard to be Benedick, all bluster and ego, but Aaron can't quite stop feeling Charlie's rib cage under his hand. Benedick wants to talk about himself, and Aaron just wants to profess his love and get to work on that corset. I suppose it's a toss-up as to which of us gets the semi during the scene.

I avoid Charlie backstage like she's paparazzi with swine flu. Because if we talk backstage, Aaron's going to take over, and I don't know if I'll be able to find Benedick again, even though I swear he was just here.

Except in Act 3, one of us does disappear. Benedick is moping around and feigns a toothache. All his friends make fun of him, and he takes Leonato aside to tell him something where "these hobbyhorses" can't hear him.

Al and I have always ad-libbed under our breaths as we walk offstage, in voices so low that only we can hear. In weeks past, I've said things to him like, "I'faith, sir, the sausage thou hadst at thy luncheon dost give thee breath that reeketh like the grave," and he's said, "Truly did the tabloids take thy measure correctly, as thou art far too light i'the loafers to have a genuine interest in my curst niece." Stuff like this.

Tonight, though, this comes out of my mouth. Or Benedick's: "I'faith, Leonato, I do love her."

"Tellst thou me something I do not already know next time," Leonato says.

From the wings, I watch the action onstage as Charlie/ Beatrice mopes around and her friends tease her. She walks right past me on her way backstage, and we look at each other and say nothing.

Intermission comes after Act 3, and the audience is making happy buzzing sounds. They've been laughing in all the right places, so we knew we were doing something right, but the intermission sounds they make just confirm what we all suspect: something special is happening here.

The cast is dead silent during intermission. We are a superstitious bunch, and just like nobody talks to a pitcher while he's in the midst of a no-hitter, nobody here wants to break the spell by talking.

This is the really cruel part of acting. We don't want to break the spell, because we have no idea how we're weaving it. Yeah, you have to be competent, know your lines and your blocking and all of that, but a really good performance is just magic. Since we don't know where magic comes from, we don't want to do anything that might make it go away, which is why I don't run over to Charlie and say we have to talk about this right now, I can't sleep and I can't eat and it's getting almost impossible for me to deny how I feel about you.

I see Charlie backstage. She looks up at me and then looks away. Is she blushing? Am I?

Act 4, and Kyanna/Hero is falsely denounced as having cheated on Claudio. I swear Al/Leonato has real tears in his eyes as he cries, after his daughter's wedding and reputation are ruined, "Hath no man's dagger here a point for me?"

I turn away because I can't stand to see him in so much

pain. I mean, Benedick turns away. He's never done that before.

And then, soon after, Beatrice and I are alone on the stage. I know the whole thing was a setup, and I'm sure Don John was involved. I feel bad for Hero, and for Leonato, and yet I can't keep my mind on their problems. My heart is racing like I've just had a triple espresso as I look into the eyes of the woman who drives me nuts more than anyone else, the woman I can't stand, the woman I can't help loving.

And then something happens that's never really happened before. Benedick goes back to the back of my brain and watches Aaron use his words to talk to Charlie.

"I . . ." Suddenly my throat is dry, and I'm sure the pounding of my heart is distracting to both Charlie and the audience. "I do love nothing in the world so well as you. Is that . . . is that not strange?"

Charlie looks at me. Beatrice is not here. She's got tears in her eyes. "I was about to protest I loved you!"

Our blocking calls for us to be delivering these lines from across the stage, still playing coy. Flannery was very clear that we're not to so much as touch during this scene, because we have to leave the audience wanting something in Act 5. She even cut my line "I will kiss your hand" at the end of the scene after I've agreed to kill Claudio, insisting that even that relatively chaste kiss would undermine the end of the play.

Screw that. My brain is going to explode if I don't touch

Charlie right now. I run to her and take her hand. "And do it with all thy heart."

The tears are streaming down Charlie's face, her mascara making black trails down her cheeks that can surely be seen even from the cheap seats. "I love you . . . ," she starts, catches her breath, and starts again, her voice quiet, breathy, and heavy with feeling. "I love you with so much of my heart, that none is left to protest."

She looks at her feet and I see a tear splat on the stage. Gently I place a hand under her chin and lift her face up. Against the director's orders, throwing professionalism to the wind, and happier than I've ever been, I pull Charlie to me and kiss her hungrily for a long time.

23

FINALLY FOUND YOU

CHARLIE

I haven't traveled on my own much. With the grueling *Jenna &
Jonah* taping schedule and the built-in travel, I never got the
chance. Plus, it was easier to just get on the plane someone
else had booked and float from one country to the next, singing the same songs to crowds I couldn't even see with the
harsh stage light. I hardly noticed the changing landscape
because all the hotel rooms looked the same. I still slept by
myself and left the video channel on all night for company.

Now, when I see the stage from the sidelines, I can also
see glimpses of the audience. Real faces. Real people waiting
to see a true play, an actual performance. And the stage itself
feels bigger than a continent. The only thing that makes it
seem at all crossable is the fact that Aaron's on the other
side. He looks at me and any distance is swallowed up. All
those moments when we had the double spotlight on us in
fake moonlight, with poorly painted sets behind us; all the

crushing crowds in Japan; the sappy songs and strained dialogue—they all rush out at me and it's easy to think about the future, even though I should be focused on what's happening right now.

I imagine years have passed, and though I've gone on to win a Golden Globe for my portrayal of a formerly slutty teen who befriends a boy with Asperger's, and produced a single album that went on to achieve critical and cult status if not commercial acclaim, and adopted a half Newfoundland, half flat-coated retriever named Moo (gracing the cover of the dog issue of O magazine), and even though I'm now bicoastal with a large town house in Chelsea and an even bigger house in Santa Monica, I'm in town to film the Big Reunion Show the Network has been plugging nonstop for months. Of course I don't want to retread on old *J&J* ground, but, lo and behold, Martinka, my ex-agent, had neglected to inform me of a rider clause to my ancient contract stating "the actor named herein is obligated to reprise this role now or in the future for digital media or rebroadcast packaging." That pretty much meant I'd have to do commentary on a couple more shows, which I did via satellite from New York, and now appear on the live reunion show. I'm not happy about all this, of course, because it takes me away from my work and from Moo, who needs daily brushing, but mainly I'm not thrilled because it means I have to come face-to-face with Aaron Whatever-his-last-name-is-now, the screenwriter of the straight-to-DVD must-miss *Call Me Intellectual* and its even worse sequel *A Real Man*, based on his novel *Just a Cincinnati Kid*, which I never read, even when I found it in the dollar remainder bin at the Strand. I've avoided his gracefully aging face, the products he hawks, and his low-point arrest/addiction caught on some tween's phone. But I can't avoid him forever.

Or maybe I'll have a different future. I don't have a Golden Globe and I never made an album because no record studio would take a chance on me after I ditched the Family Network and ground my career to a halt when scathing reviews were posted online from critics watching *Much Ado*, Twittering in the seats as they watched. And maybe I have to live in two cities because I'm so busy chasing down auditions even for kitty-litter ads and regional shoe stores and, even worse, I have to appear at conventions with other used-to-be-famous people from old sitcoms or bad movies. I do things like open Big Mitch's Used Auto Lot in Branford, Connecticut, and cut the ribbon on the new multiplex in Culver, Indiana, and even in Culver only a handful of people show up to have me sign their old *Jenna & Jonah* mugs or T-shirts.

Or maybe none of this happens. What does *Acting from Within* say? *Imagine the present as you want it, create the future as you need it to be, act from within.*

Maybe a different future is just beginning as I step onstage now. The lights flare and suddenly I'm not me anymore, I'm Beatrice. Her hand motions are not my own, so when she gestures for Benedick to back off, I don't feel as though it's purely my doing. And when I dance with a stranger at the masked ball, I actually forget the stranger is Benedick. I forget this and allow this because when the lights came up and the audience hushed themselves, part of me clicked on and that part is an actor. Someone more than capable of slipping into another person's skin and finding her feelings. And I'm only able to do this because I have finally, finally found my own feelings. What did Al say? The best actors are self-aware; they know their limitations, their foibles, and are open to surprises. My years on television might not have given me the ability to cry on command, but my work ethic is intact. And the news scandal might not have made me look like the most bankable, honest star, but it showed I was able to pull a fast one on millions. That my costar and I were good fakers.

But now I'm not faking.

So while Beatrice and Benedick spar their way through the scenes on the huge stage, causing laughter to spurt from the audience in audible waves, Aaron and I are locked in more than just a battle of wits. We are locked in the present day with our true feelings. He says his line about his horse and I can't do anything but stare at the artfully painted fake sky, because I know if I look at him he'll know. And I can't have him know, because it's ridiculous, really. To want someone you've already kissed hundreds of times to kiss you for the first time.

When he moves forward toward me, I know we're

supposed to end the scene, but I don't want to do it. I see why actors want to do the same play every night for months at a time. Each night you find yourself living the role; each time your skin stretches just a little bit.

I've been acting for real—giving my best-ever performance tonight—and I inject another life into Beatrice, give her a present she never had. The gift of being able to go after what I feel and what fits. But before Aaron's character and mine cling together, I feel something else. My eyes fill and, before I can control them, tears come spilling down my cheeks. Benedick asks why the sadness comes forth and I have to tell him. And when the play ends, I'm sure he'll know. But where he might have made fun of me for it before, he's gentle with me now as I wipe my eyes with my fingertips.

"Who knew you were capable of tears?" he whispers during our bow.

I turn to him and address him in my regular voice. "It turns out I can cry after all. I just never had anything so terrible to picture that made me go to that dark place."

Aaron smirks, caught between reaching for my hand and worrying that this whole thing is a gag for the nonexistent cameras. But it couldn't be any less of a joke. "And now you do?"

I whisper to him. "All I could picture was, what if after this scene or act or play ends, I never see you again. I pictured being away from you, or being pulled away from you, and it felt like I was being torn in half."

The audience quits their clapping, falling completely silent to hear us.

"I was acting Beatrice," I say.

"And doing a brilliant job!" shouts someone from the audience. The people who have already left their seats stop moving toward the exits.

"But it isn't just because I've always loved this play. Or because I got whipped into shape by you, Al. Or by the biggest director in the smallest shoes." I take Aaron's hand and look into his eyes. "All this time I thought there was the Jenna me and the regular me. And the me that did crummy commercials for shoes that made kids' feet hurt. Or hocked power bars that contained things like dextramethalizionanese, and then another self that stood on tiptoes to kiss you at the farmer's market. And another one who could put on a corset and say words that have existed for hundreds of years. But it turns out those are all the same person. All me. All aspects of who I am at any given time and how being a good actor means knowing yourself—knowing that you have a whole person to go back to."

"And where is that person going?" Aaron asks, withdrawing his hand as a question.

"Yeah, where are you going, Jenna?" shouts someone from the darkness.

Cameras rush to the stage for a close-up and a microphone is thrust into my hand by a tall guy with a press pass. Bret Huckley's evil cackle and multiple camera clicks invade.

"Can you address rumors about your relationship?"

"Is it true that *Jenna & Jonah's How to Be a Rock Star* is being made into a motion picture with younger stars to launch a whole new cast for a future show?"

"Where exactly are you two headed after this? Will you do a reunion show?"

But this play hasn't been a reunion show. And we haven't been apart for years. And a reunion show, if we ever do one, is years and parts and travels away. For now, all I know is that I can act. I can cry. I found love and, with it, found myself. And Aaron, the man standing next to me, is my old friend and my new love wrapped into one. Whatever he does next, and whatever part I get when I leave here, the roles we want aren't necessarily together on-screen. But offscreen, facing the crowds and cast, with our past piled up in episodes and our futures uncertain, we're just like that Jenna and Jonah song that got cut from the closing credits. Aaron and I pushed for it—it was acoustic and real, just us singing "Starstruck with Each Other" with no background singers or amped-up effects—but the powers that be yanked it, said it was too simplistic to work. It is simple, isn't it?

I turn to face Aaron and he puts his hand to his heart, the ultimate gesture of love, and I don't fight the smile that slicks itself across my face. He pulls my hand to his lips and then I pull him close to me so we can kiss until midnight or morning, until the lights fade out and the audience goes home.

ACKNOWLEDGMENTS

A Big Hollywood thank-you to: my tofu-loving coauthor; Faye and Doug; Emily and Mary Kate and the crew at Walker; and my own home-based entourage, N. S. (camera and cue cards), S. S. (head of music dept.), E. S. (wardrobe and decoration), A. S. (props and language), A. J. S. (leading man and so much more). And, of course, Hooter Von Binken and the entire Smythe-Bauxregaurde family. —E. F.

Big Thanks to The Authentic People's Pleasure Company and La Comedia Dinner Theater; Suzanne, Casey, Rowen, and Kylie; Emily; Emily again, but a different one this time; Doug; Faye; Mary Kate; Ula Cafe; and Seamus Cooper. —B. H.